A slip of the tongue . . .

"Why don't you go try this stuff on?" Joanna said.

"Okay." Abby took the sandals from Joanna. "I'm gonna go change in Kristen's room and make a grand entrance." She crossed the room quickly. "I can't wait until Greg sees me in this. He's gonna just die."

"Greg?" Joanna asked. "You mean Will, right?"

Abby stopped in her tracks and felt a rush of heat rise up her neck. Why had she said Greg?

"Ab?"

"Uh, of course I meant Will. I just, uh, Greg's coming over to see what I picked out." Even as she said it, Abby knew the excuse sounded lame.

"Uh huh," Kristen said sarcastically. "That's *exactly* it."

Abby walked into Kristen's tiny room. She shut the door behind her and sat down shakily on the cot, feeling almost faint.

Greg.

Greg was her best friend. The thought of him wasn't actually making her skin tingle and her knees all mushy, was it?

Kiss
and Tell

Kieran Scott

BANTAM BOOKS
NEW YORK • TORONTO • LONDON • SYDNEY • AUCKLAND

*To Dad and Ian, the only people more psyched
about these books than me.*

RL 6, age 12 and up

KISS AND TELL

A Bantam Book / July 1998

Produced by Daniel Weiss Associates, Inc.
33 West 17th Street
New York, NY 10011.
Cover photography by Michael Segal.

ISBN: 0-553-49251-9

Published simultaneously in the United States and Canada

Bantam Books are published by Bantam Books, a division of Bantam
Doubleday Dell Publishing Group, Inc. Its trademark, consisting of the
words "Bantam Books" and the portrayal of a rooster, is Registered in
U.S. Patent and Trademark Office and in other countries. Marca
Registrada. Bantam Books, 1540 Broadway, New York, New York 10036.

PRINTED IN THE UNITED STATES OF AMERICA

OPM   0 9 8 7 6 5 4 3 2 1

One

ABBY STEWART CLOMPED through the door of her cabin at Camp Emerson, dropped her bags on the wood plank floor, and inhaled deeply. Ah! The smell of musty mattresses, bug spray, and fresh mountain air. It was like coming home.

"Abby!"

Manisha Tare grabbed Abby up in a hug and spun her around.

"Hey, Manny!" Abby said with a grin. "Did you grow, like, five feet?" she asked, looking *up* at Manisha for the first time in the seven years they'd known each other. Manisha now towered over her.

"I wouldn't say five feet," Manisha responded, running a hand through her short black curls. "But I could probably beat you in basketball now."

"We'll see about that." Abby laughed.

Manisha grabbed Abby's suitcase and Abby lifted her backpack, turning left into one of the two bunk rooms in the cabin. There were three cots along the walls of the room, each with a small table and dresser next to it and each sporting a bright orange cotton blanket with the name of the cabin—Birchwood—stamped across it in army green.

"Even Birchwood has these ugly things?" Abby lamented, flinging her bag on an unclaimed cot.

"I know. It's such a fashion faux pas," Manisha joked. "But aren't you glad we got Birchwood? It's like we finally made it."

"Seniors!" Abby cheered, playfully slapping five with Manisha.

The two girls ran to the window at the back of the cabin and looked out. Abby smiled brightly. Birchwood was always reserved for one set of senior campers at Camp Emerson, and she and her friends had spent the entire school year praying that they would be the ones to get it. It was the biggest cabin, the closest to all the common areas, and had an incredible view of Lake Emerson and the mountains behind it.

Abby pulled the rubber band out of her hair, letting her long brown waves fall over her shoulders. It was time to relax. "Is everybody here already?" she asked, stretching her arms above her head.

"Allyson, Shira, and Jeannie are here, but they went over to Arapaho to see the rest of the crew," Manisha said. "Oh—Allyson chopped her hair off! It looks great."

"No way!" Abby exclaimed. "We're talking short?"

"We're talking above-the-ear short," Manisha confirmed with a nod.

"Unreal!" Allyson's auburn hair had been down to her butt for as long as Abby could remember. Abby shook her head. Her friends sure had done some changing this year.

"So where's Joanna?" Manisha asked, sitting down on her cot.

"Late as usual," Abby said with a wry smile. At least *that* hadn't changed. Abby's best camp friend, Joanna Klein, had never been on time for anything in her life. Every year Abby spent her first hour at camp waiting in the parking lot for Joanna to show up in her parents' limousine. "I'm gonna go back and wait for her. Do ya wanna come?"

"Nah. I think I'll just get settled," Manisha said.

"Cool. I'll catch you later, then."

"Later!" Manisha called.

Once outside, Abby lifted her already tanned face to the sun and smiled contentedly. This was going to be the best summer ever. Abby and her friends always loved camp, but as senior campers they'd finally be allowed to pick a "major program" and a "minor program" and avoid most of the lame tree hugging, arts and crafts, and undesirable sports they were forced to do in the past. Abby planned to spend the entire summer improving her soccer skills so that she could walk right onto the varsity team in the fall and kick butt in a major way.

"And to top it all off, Greg Neill, anticamp spokesman of America, is on the guys' side right now, unpacking his duffel bag," Abby whispered to herself, still smiling. Abby had pulled off a major coup when she'd persuaded her best friend from home, Greg Neill, to join her at good old Emerson this summer.

Abby almost laughed out loud as she walked along the path back to the parking lot, where counselors were still greeting latecomers. Greg usually spent his summers at the local pool in their hometown of Passmore, Delaware. But this year Abby had convinced him to put his exciting splash war plans on hold. It had taken a bit of wheedling, but when Abby had explained that the senior campers got to choose their program and had reminded him that the head soccer instructor was a former Olympian, Greg began to beg his parents to send him to camp.

Greg had spent the entire bus ride from Passmore to Emerson, Pennsylvania, whining about the trip, but Abby knew he was just as psyched as she was to get to camp and start working out.

Suddenly Abby caught sight of a shiny black stretch limo pulling into the parking lot. Joanna—it had to be.

Abby ran over to the car just as Joanna was emerging from the backseat. Then she did something she'd only do for Joanna—she squealed.

"Jo!"

"Hey, girl!"

Abby wrapped her arms around Joanna's slim frame, hugging her tightly before pulling back to get a better look at her. Joanna's short red hair was cut in a shag, and she was wearing a crisp white blouse and denim shorts. Perfect as always.

"You look great!" they both said at the same time.

"You're late, Klein," Abby said in a stern voice.

"Thanks for the news flash," Joanna responded, rolling her eyes. "You wouldn't believe the traffic—"

"Miss Klein?" Joanna's chauffeur stood next to the driver's side door of the limo. He was a tall, formal-looking young man, wearing a classic gray uniform. "Would you mind if I ran inside for a moment and used the . . . uh . . . facilities?"

Abby stifled a giggle.

"Sure, James. You don't have to ask," Joanna said, a hint of amusement in her voice.

James blushed. "Thanks, Miss Klein." He turned and hurried off toward the main cabin.

"He's new," Joanna said, shrugging.

"He's cute," Abby teased.

"Speaking of cute," Joanna said, her green eyes sparkling. "Did you see Teddy yet?"

"Color me drooling," Abby confirmed. Teddy Barber was the camp director's son, and he'd been the headliner of every daydream of the female Emerson population for years. He was twenty now, but he'd officially become worship worthy when he was just fourteen and had saved one of Abby's friends from drowning in the lake. Abby shook her head. "There's no way he's really related to that freak of nature Babs."

Joanna's eyes focused on something behind

Abby, and her face suddenly went ashen.

Abby's heart plummeted. From Joanna's expression she could tell that Babs—also known as Mrs. Barber—the camp director, was standing right behind her.

"Hello, Ms. Stewart!" a voice bellowed out.

Yep. There was no mistaking that unfeminine baritone. Abby turned slowly and looked right up into Babs's ruddy face. She was wearing her usual camp uniform: tan shorts, tan Camp Emerson T-shirt, knee-high socks, and a baseball cap. As always, a shiny silver whistle on a bright red rope hung around her neck.

"Hi, Babs!" Abby said cheerfully, trying to cover up her overwhelming embarrassment.

"Don't worry, Stewy," Babs said, slapping Abby on the shoulder. "I'll let ya off this time. But why don't you girls get this car unpacked and get the show on the road." Babs patted Joanna's trunk twice and then continued on her way to the top of the drive, calling greetings to campers as she went.

"You can breathe now," Joanna said when Babs was out of earshot.

"Thanks," Abby said, letting out a whoosh of air. "She must be in a good mood, or I'd already be cleaning bathrooms." She grinned. Everyone knew that Babs only talked tough. She hardly ever enforced a punishment on anybody. "All right, you heard the woman," Abby said, mocking Babs's deep voice. "Let's get you unpacked." Abby paused for a moment and looked over at the trunk. "What did you do—pack the entire J. Crew summer collection in here?"

"Very funny," Joanna said.

"Seriously. I work out every day, and I still don't think I can lift this thing," she said, pulling tentatively on one of the handles.

"What do you mean?" Joanna asked, her eyes wide with astonishment. "I was counting on my athletic best friend to do all the grunt work!"

Abby laughed. This was their seventh year at Camp Emerson together, and Joanna never failed to surprise Abby with the amount of junk she brought with her from New York City. Abby, on the other hand, had arrived carrying one suitcase, a backpack, and her good-luck charm—a lovingly battered soccer ball.

"Why didn't you just rent a U-Haul?" Abby joked, leaning over to untie the thick rope that held Joanna's megacase in the trunk of the limo. She jumped back as the trunk popped up.

"Please, Abby. Like I'd be caught dead in a U-Haul," Joanna said merrily.

"C'mon, don't just stand there," Abby said. "You hafta help me with this thing."

Joanna shrugged. "I don't know how much help I'll be." She pushed up her pristine white sleeves and walked over to the opposite end of the trunk.

Abby removed the rubber band from her wrist, pulled her hair back into a ponytail, and took a deep breath. "Okay, just grab ahold of the handle and ease it to the ground," she directed.

Joanna looked dubious. "Why don't we just wait for James? And where's your friend Greg, anyway?" she asked, raising her perfectly plucked eyebrows hopefully. "He could help us."

Abby laughed and crouched down to tighten the lace on her high-top sneaker. "Sorry, he's over on the guys' side, bonding with all the other manly men." She cocked her head toward the lake at the center of camp, which separated the boys' cabins from the girls'. "Besides, don't you want to freshen up before you meet him for the first time?"

Joanna looked startled. She reached into her little leather purse and pulled out a tiny mirror. "Do I look that bad?" she asked as she examined her perfect ivory complexion.

"You won't be winning any beauty contests," Abby lied, trying not to giggle. In all honesty, Abby thought that if the Miss Teen USA scouts showed up at Camp Emerson at that very moment, they would swoop down on Joanna like hawks after their prey. In fact, they'd probably trample over Abby in her blue Adidas shorts and oversize white T-shirt in their rush to get to Joanna. But Abby didn't have to tell her that.

"Well, it doesn't matter, anyway," Joanna said finally, replacing the mirror and closing her purse with a snap. "I have plenty of time to reinvent myself before dinner."

"Like you really need reinventing," Abby scoffed, smiling at Joanna.

"Okay, Ab," Joanna said. "If we're gonna do this, let's get it over with."

"Right." Abby grasped the handle on the large case again. "On the count of three. One . . . two . . . three!"

Abby yanked up on the handle and was surprised to find that the box was lighter than she expected. She lifted her side easily, but Joanna dropped her end with a thud, causing a cloud of dust to rise up around the trunk.

"Sorry," Joanna said, examining her hands. "I didn't know it was going to be so heavy."

Abby smiled. She was still holding her end at waist level. "Why don't you go see if you can find Kristen to help me carry this thing up to the cabin?" she suggested.

"That's why you're the smart one!" Joanna said, taking off for the area at the top of the drive where the counselors were greeting late campers.

Kristen Datolli was the counselor in charge of Birchwood and would also be the assistant soccer instructor this year. Abby had always admired Kristen's sense of humor, easygoing nature, and total poise on the soccer field. She was psyched to study Kristen's every move this summer to get some pointers for her own game.

"Earth to Abby!" A pair of tan fingers suddenly snapped in front of her face. "Joanna tells me you need some help."

"Oh! Hey, Kristen," Abby said, smiling. "How's the counselor thing going?"

"Fine so far," Kristen answered, pulling the brim of her well-worn Yankees baseball cap lower over her brow. "I'm glad I got you guys this year. Some of those younger kids are such whiners."

Abby laughed as Kristen rounded the other side of Joanna's trunk and bent at her knees to get a grip on the handle. Joanna stood behind Kristen with her arms crossed over her chest, watching with a furrowed brow as if she were concentrating on an algebra problem.

"Okay, on three," Abby directed again. "One . . . two . . ."

"Three!" Kristen cried, lifting her side of the case easily. At that exact moment Abby saw something that made her heart stand still. There, across the parking lot, was the most beautiful guy she had ever laid eyes on. He had light brown hair pulled back in a ponytail, chiseled features, and a body that boasted of a thousand tough workouts. He was leaning back against the hood of a sleek red sports car, wearing khaki shorts and a blue polo, chatting with Babs.

Abby's mouth gaped open, and she dropped the trunk on her toe. "Yow!" she screamed, pulling her wounded foot out from under the trunk. She slapped her hand over her mouth, hoping the ponytail man hadn't heard her.

"Are you all right?" Joanna asked. She rushed over as Abby bounced around on her good leg, shaking her free hand in front of her frantically. Finally Abby sat down on the trunk and pulled off her sneaker.

"Do you want some ice?" Kristen asked with

concern, kneeling on the ground next to Abby.

"Did you *see* that guy?" Abby asked, rubbing her toe as she tried to see over Kristen.

"Huh?" Joanna squinted around at the few people left in the lot. "What guy?"

"Are you in pain or not?" Kristen demanded. "I *am* responsible for you now, you know."

"Ma'am, yes, ma'am. I am in pain, ma'am," Abby said. "But who cares? I think I'm in love."

"She's delusional," Joanna told Kristen.

Kristen's eyebrows shot up. "With who?" she asked Abby.

Abby looked over Kristen's head and found the guy she was looking for. Babs said something that made the gorgeous boy laugh, and the sound carried to Abby's ears, sending a chill down her spine.

"Him! That new guy. Is he a counselor, Kristen?" Abby asked, pointing to the ponytail man.

Kristen shook her head. "Never seen him before."

"I don't believe it. A new guy, our age, who's not Greg. What are the chances of that?" Abby wondered aloud. "Is he not perfection personified?"

"Perfection personified?" Kristen repeated. "Since when do you talk like *YM* magazine?"

"Oh, no," Joanna suddenly said quietly.

"What?" Abby asked, her heart skipping a beat at the tone in Joanna's voice—clearly there was something about the new guy that Joanna didn't like. She sounded like someone had just told her she'd have to give up her favorite platform sandals.

"Oh, no," Joanna repeated, her voice growing louder. "This is *so* not happening."

"What?" Abby and Kristen asked in unison.

"Please tell me this is not happening," Joanna said again. She brought her hands to her face and peeked through her fingers in the direction of the car.

"*What?*" Abby and Kristen shouted. Joanna was given to fits of drama. She was an actress—it was in her nature.

"That's Will Stevenson," Joanna said finally, looking at Abby's ponytail man with a bit of a sneer.

"You *know* him?" Abby shrieked.

"Yeah. And he's nothing to get all psyched over," Joanna scoffed. "He's a total egomaniac. Major attitude with nothing to back it up."

"Coulda fooled me," Kristen said, looking Will up and down. "I'd say he has a *lot* to brag about."

"Hey!" Abby protested, sitting up straight. "I saw him first!"

"No. *I* saw him first," Joanna said. "And trust me, I am *not* happy to be seeing him again."

"Okay, give," Abby demanded, wiggling her toes inside her sweat sock to test for pain. "How do you know him?"

"'Member when I told you about that walk-on part I was doing for *Sunrise Island*?" Joanna asked, plopping down on the trunk next to Abby.

"Yeah. You said your agent was excited because

they were going to let you read for a small role on the soap if they liked your look," Abby said.

Joanna was forever auditioning for off-Broadway plays, TV pilots, and soap operas. So far she had walked across the set of at least ten soaps and had three lines on a pilot called *Girls in Space*.

"Well, Will Stevenson totally ruined my shot at stardom," Joanna said, gesturing grandly in Will's direction. "All we were supposed to do was walk across the soundstage together and pretend to be talking, but Will the Great spent the entire day jockeying for camera time."

"Jockeying for camera time?" Kristen asked.

"He blocked her out of the shot," Abby explained. She'd heard enough of Joanna's showbiz stories to have the lingo down solid.

"Right," Joanna said with a curt nod. "So guess who got to read for the directors instead of me?" She crossed her legs and bounced her foot up and down in obvious frustration.

"Will Stevenson?" Abby asked, looking him over once more. He was just sliding into the passenger's seat of the car. Abby noticed the driver for the first time—an older version of Will, who must be his father. She saw Will lean across the console and turn up the volume on the radio. He and his dad both sang along to a classic rock tune as the car peeled onto the road, probably heading for the guys' side of camp. Abby laughed.

"What's so funny?" Joanna demanded.

"He doesn't look evil," Abby said with a smile.

"Whatever, Ab," Joanna said, sounding almost angry. "Trust your hormones over your best friend. See if I care. But don't come running to me when your brain melts out your ear from hearing him talk about himself so much." Joanna stood, slapped her hands against her denim shorts, and pulled a pair of black cat-eye sunglasses out of her pocket.

"He's so full of himself, I'm surprised he hasn't choked on his own attitude," Joanna continued quietly, staring at the bend in the road around which Will's car had disappeared.

Abby shoved her foot back into her sneaker and tied the laces. "Full of himself?" she asked, standing up and resting her chin on Joanna's shoulder from behind. "Unlike you?"

"That's different," Joanna said without missing a beat. "I deserve to be cocky. I'm perfect."

Abby and Joanna both laughed.

"Ahem," Kristen interrupted. "Now that we've established that Joanna is perfect and Will is decidedly not, and that Abby is going to do whatever she wants, anyway—which we already knew—can we move this monster trunk so I can get back to work?"

"Slave driver," Abby quipped. She bent over and easily lifted the trunk with Kristen. Joanna slung her backpack over one shoulder and used her other hand to pull her large suitcase along the bumpy trail on its wheels.

James was running back to the car just as they began moving. "Miss Klein, let me," he called worriedly as he ran.

"That's all right, James," Joanna told him, waving him away. "They got it."

Kristen grinned. "It's good to see you haven't changed," she remarked.

"I work hard on that," Joanna responded. "Drive safely, James," she called over her shoulder.

"Thank you, Miss Klein. Take care," James bellowed back.

As they walked, Kristen started to tell Abby and Joanna about the hassle Jeannie Yu's chronically overprotective parents had caused when they'd arrived to move her in earlier that day. It was an old story—it happened every year. Abby tuned her out. All she could think about was Will. Kristen was right; no matter what Joanna said, Abby would make up her own mind about Will once she had a chance to hang out with him.

One thing's for sure, Abby thought, grinning, *I can't wait to start my research.*

TWO

GREG NEILL LEANED back on his flimsy-looking cot in his new home away from home, a smelly cabin called Matawan. The mattress was lumpy, and the pillow was a thin slab of foam.

"So much for sleep," he muttered, tucking his hands behind his head. "I wonder why Abby forgot to mention the whole anticomfort thing they've got going on here."

He glanced around the bunk. There were four metal-frame beds in the small room, and each was strewn with backpacks, baseball caps, clothing, and an array of CDs and Walkman disc players. The cabin housed eight campers, four more in another room the same size, and one counselor, whose room was marked off by half walls in between the two bunk rooms. Maybe once everyone had really settled in, the cabin would start to feel more like a home.

Greg sighed, stood up, and grabbed his soccer ball

from under the bed. At least his bunk mates had seemed cool. Two of them, Simon and Dominic, had been coming to Emerson forever and were obviously best friends. When Greg had first walked into the bunk, they'd given him the cold shoulder, marking him as an outsider. But once they'd found out he was here for the soccer program and that he was friends with Abby, they'd warmed right up.

Greg stood in the center of the room and started juggling the ball with his feet and knees, counting out loud as he played. Even though the guys had started to accept him, he was glad to have some time alone to decompress after the long trip. Greg had arrived later than the others, and Matawan's counselor, Damon Fields, had told Greg he could finish unpacking and wait at the cabin for their last bunk mate while everyone else headed over to the mess hall for dinner.

"Eighty . . . eighty-one . . . eighty-two . . . ," Greg counted as he concentrated on the ball. A few more touches and he would break a hundred without letting the ball touch the ground.

"Ninety-two . . . ninety-three . . ." Sweat broke out on Greg's forehead as his green eyes followed the ball. His foot, his knee, his chest, his foot. Almost there. "Ninety-six . . . ninety-seven . . ."

"Home, sweet home!" A big guy with a long brown ponytail flung open the door with a bang just as Greg reached ninety-nine.

Thwack!

The ball hit the top of Greg's foot at a bad angle,

and it rocketed through the air toward the newcomer.

"Whoa!" the new guy yelped as he jumped out of the way.

Bam! The ball slammed into the wall next to the door, and a skateboard leaning up against the wall fell over with a crash.

"Is that the way you greet all your bunk mates?" the new guy asked.

Greg tried to push aside his frustration. He'd been so close. . . . He forcibly relaxed his features and ran a hand through his scruffy blond hair, scratching at the damp nape of his neck.

"Sorry, man," he said, flashing a smile. "I guess I shouldn't play in the house."

"No harm done," the new guy said. He dropped a large canvas duffel bag on the floor and offered his hand. "Name's Stevenson, Will Stevenson."

Greg laughed and returned Will's firm handshake. "What're you, double-o-six or double-o-eight?" he asked.

Will didn't laugh. He didn't even smile.

"You know—Bond, James Bond?" Greg asked, hoping to clarify his joke.

"I get it," Will said stiffly. He grabbed his bag and crossed to the only bed that wasn't already taken.

Okay, Greg thought. *Obviously no sense of humor on this guy.*

"I'm Greg," he said, sitting down on his cot—the one right next to Will's. He wondered if he could get one of the other guys to switch beds with him. A summer next to this uptight guy was not Greg's idea of a good time.

"Nice to meet you," Will grunted, keeping his back to Greg as he unzipped his bag and started to remove neatly folded stacks of clothing—polos, sweater vests, and wrinkle-free chinos. Even his denim shorts looked like they'd been pressed.

"So, what program are you here for?" Greg asked.

"Drama," Will answered, turning to face Greg. He was actually smiling now. "I heard the new instructor here was from the drama department at Yale, which is one of the best in the country. I want to get in there when I graduate, so I figured . . . might as well start early."

Greg tried to look impressed, but acting was not exactly something he could relate to. "Where're you from?" he asked.

"Manhattan," Will answered. "This is my first time here."

"Me too," Greg said, happy they had *something* in common. "I'm from Delaware, by the way. I've never been to camp at all."

"Me neither," Will said. "I hope it doesn't stink. You know, I hear they're always telling you when to eat, when to sleep. They probably even assign times for you to use the bathroom," he said with a laugh.

Greg relaxed a little. So the guy did have a sense of humor—sort of. He lay back on his bed and put his hands behind his head. "This place is supposed to be pretty cool, though," he said, studying some of the graffiti etched in the beam above his head. *Whitesnake Rules*. Okay. So maybe they'd have to update the decor a little.

"Really?" Will asked, shoving his empty duffel bag underneath his bed and sitting down on the orange cotton blanket with a creak. "Where'd you hear that?"

"My best friend Abby's been coming here for years," Greg explained. "She says they're really loose with the older groups—scheduling free time, letting us choose our evening activities. And our counselor, Damon, seems pretty cool. Even though he's a little . . . uh-oh." Greg's stomach flipped as he glanced at his watch.

"What?" Will asked.

"We gotta go, man." Greg jumped up, crossed the cabin in one long stride, and yanked open the squeaky screen door.

"What's up?" Will asked, following at Greg's heels as he ran down the steps and took off at a jog.

It was just starting to get dark. Greg was glad the layout of the camp was fairly simple. Abby would never let him forget it if he got lost. "I told Damon I'd wait for the last guy to show up so he could take everyone else to the mess hall," Greg explained, his rubber-soled sneakers thudding against the packed dirt path that led to the common buildings.

"I guess I'm the last guy," Will said, matching Greg's pace.

"And I said I'd get you to dinner as soon as you got here," Greg said. He hurdled a large branch and sidestepped a rock.

"Hope we didn't miss it," Will commented. "I'm starved."

"Me too," Greg said, feeling the grumble in his stomach as he bounded up the rickety plank steps to the mess cabin.

As he slid through the door into the noisy mess hall he instantly remembered the main reason he'd been worried about coming to camp: food. Food was one of Greg's favorite things in the entire world, and as a little eight-year-old with spiked hair walked by holding a tray full of glop, Greg had a feeling he'd be finding a way to smuggle pizzas through the front gate—soon.

"1-800-DOMINOS?" Will asked.

"You read my mind, man," Greg said.

"Ugh! That's nasty!" Will groaned, eyeing a blackened hot dog that had found its way to the newly shined linoleum floor.

Greg was about to agree when he felt a firm hand on his back.

"Where ya been, Neill?"

Greg turned and found himself face-to-face with Damon Fields. Damon was shorter than Greg's nearly six feet, but he was as broad as an NFL linebacker—not the type of guy Greg wanted to make angry. He was wearing a tight white T-shirt that stretched over his considerable muscles and contrasted starkly with his deep ebony skin. Obviously Damon wanted to give his campers the impression that he wasn't to be messed with.

"Hey, Damon," Greg said calmly. "This is Will Stevenson."

"Hi," Will said, extending his arm.

"Hey, man," Damon replied, grasping Will's hand quickly. "Hope you won't be this late for everything. You guys hear this is a loose camp and you think there won't be any rules, but that's not the way I run my cabin. Got it?" Damon crossed his arms over his chest and placed his hands in his armpits, making his biceps look even bigger.

"I thought you said he was cool," Will whispered out of the corner of his mouth.

"I am cool." Damon walked around behind the two campers. Will blushed to the color of a watermelon. "I just like to make wimps like you two squirm," Damon said good-naturedly, slapping each of them on the back. Greg had to struggle not to yelp, and Will hopped forward a few steps from the force of Damon's slap. Even though Damon's attitude was jovial, the point of these love taps was clear—Damon is king.

"Anyway," Damon said. "Grab some grub. There's no more room at our table, so you two lovelies are going to have to sit with the girls for all your meals this summer. That's your punishment for being late."

Greg's eyebrows shot up. Sit with the girls? That sounded more like a pleasure than a punishment. He scanned the room for Abby or any other worthy woman to share his inaugural camp meal with. Huh. He scanned the room again. Nothing. No one. There was a table with a few girls who seemed to be his age, but there wasn't a remotely intriguing female among them. Where was Abby?

Great, Greg thought as he and Will moved toward the buffet-style food line at the front of the mess hall. *A counselor with an authority complex, charred pork sticks served on floor tile, and no eye candy in sight.* Why did he ever let Abby talk him into coming here? He could be eating his mom's gourmet roast chicken right now.

Suddenly a shriek pierced the room. "Hey! Watch . . ."

There was a multistaged crash at the front of the line: the sound of cracking ceramic, followed by the shattering of glass, ending with the sound of silverware clattering across the floor. Silence filled the room, followed slowly by hoots of laughter and applause.

Greg turned to catch a glimpse of the poor soul who had made a fool of himself. His eyes focused on the spilled meal—something leafy that might have passed for a salad—then traveled up the shapely female legs that stood above the mess. He took in the slim waist, stylish clothing, and finally the beautiful, breathtaking face.

His jaw dropped.

This girl was a goddess. A klutz, sure, but a goddess just the same.

She smiled as the laughter and clapping continued and then bent into a deep bow, swinging her arm out gracefully. She even mouthed a modest thank-you.

Who *was* this girl?

Suddenly Greg heard a familiar laugh. His eyes darted to the left and he saw Abby, giggling like crazy and patting the girl on the back. Abby knew his goddess? Greg looked back at the klutz in confusion. Wait a minute . . . no . . . it couldn't be. . . .

"Oh, no," Will said suddenly, but Greg was too mesmerized to ask what was wrong.

He studied his dream girl and realized in a rush that he was looking at the infamous Joanna Klein: Abby's redheaded, lovably obnoxious, petrified-of-spiders best friend from camp. He'd seen pictures of Joanna before, and he'd always thought she was cute, but in person . . . well . . . *wow*.

"Oh, no," Will repeated as a couple of counselors began to help Joanna clean up her mess.

"What?" Greg asked.

"I know I'm not seeing who I think I'm seeing," Will said with a sneer.

"Who?" Greg asked. "Her?" He pointed casually at Joanna, who was resuming her place in line. She was just so gorgeous. Greg could imagine her smiling beautifully as they took a private sail across the lake together—

"Yeah, *her*," Will said. "Joanna Klein."

"You know her?" Greg asked. They grabbed brown plastic trays and hopped on the end of the dwindling line.

"I met her once," Will said, snatching two burgers and dropping them onto a ceramic plate. "She's got the worst attitude going. We're talking major stuck-up snob."

"She can't be that bad," Greg said. He glanced over at the table where Abby and Joanna were sitting down. "That girl with her is my best friend, Abby. And if I'm her best friend, she obviously has good taste in people."

"Keep dreamin'." Will laughed shortly. He threw Greg a glance over his shoulder. "Seriously, man, trust me. That girl is bad news."

"Yeah, well, we're supposed to sit with the girls, so I'm going over there," Greg said. He inconspicuously checked his hair in the side of a metal napkin dispenser. It looked just like it always did—scruffy. *It'll do,* he decided with a shrug. "You can come if you want," he told Will. "But if you don't, Damon'll probably make you sit with the eight-year-olds."

"*Okay,*" Will said, picking up his tray and squaring his shoulders as if he were heading into battle. "But you're risking major indigestion."

Greg laughed and started to weave his way around the tables, chairs, and wailing kids, never taking his eyes off the beautiful Joanna. Will seemed pretty cool, but Greg wasn't about to be scared off by his comments. After all, they had just met. And Abby was his oldest friend. If she liked Joanna, Greg was sure he'd like her too.

Abby looked up and caught Greg's eye, and he smiled in greeting. Then he glanced over at Joanna again and a shiver went down his spine.

Camp was about to get interesting.

Three

"OH, NO WAY," Abby said. Her heart thudded in her chest as she struggled to chew on a rather tough piece of meat. Greg and Will were weaving their way through the room, heading straight for Abby's table.

"Oh, no way, what?" Joanna asked, glancing over her shoulder in the direction Abby was looking. She groaned and rolled her eyes.

Manisha was sitting to Abby's right, and she leaned over and nudged Abby's elbow. "He's a hottie," she said, flicking her eyes toward Greg and Will.

"I know," Abby said, grinning. "I love long hair on a guy."

"Not *him*," Manisha whispered. "The blonde."

Abby laughed. "That's my best friend, Greg. The guy I told you about."

Shira leaned across the table. "You never

mentioned he was a babe," she hissed. "We're talking Teddy Barber material."

"Seriously, Ab," Joanna added. "His pictures don't do him justice."

Abby was about to respond when one of the guys' counselors—a new guy whom Kristen had dubbed Damon the Destroyer—joined Greg and Will as they reached the far end of the table.

"Hey, loser!" Abby called out, greeting Greg in their normal fashion.

Greg nodded at her and grinned. "Hey, ugly!"

The rest of the girls at the table giggled.

"Ladies," Damon addressed them with a cocky smile. Abby looked the counselor over quickly and decided he was moderately cute—in a World Wrestling Federation kind of way. "These two campers were late to dinner," Damon continued. "We have more senior guys than girls this year, so Greg and Will here have won the distinct honor of dining with you for the duration of camp."

Jeannie, Shira, and Manisha all eyed Greg appreciatively. Abby grimaced—this was weird. She loved her bunk mates, but none of them was good enough for her best friend. Of course, Greg could hold his own. It would all be fine as long as they stayed away from Will.

Abby smiled at Joanna. "This is so cool," she said.

"Yippee," Joanna responded sarcastically. She violently tore off little bits of bread from her roll and flung them at her plate. Abby wished Joanna would lighten up. Will couldn't be *that* bad.

"Good luck, men," Damon said. He slapped Greg on the back, causing the water glass on his tray to jump.

"Well, guys, welcome to our world," Kristen said. She stood up and looked down the table toward Abby and Joanna. "There seem to be two open seats at the other end. I'm sure Abby and Jo will make you feel right at home."

"Not in this lifetime," Joanna muttered.

"Be nice," Abby warned under her breath as the guys shuffled between chairs on their way over.

She caught Will's eyes for a moment, and he smiled and nodded. *A dimple,* Abby thought. *The boy even has a dimple!* She felt a blush rising to her cheeks and looked down at her plate to compose herself.

"Um . . . Abby, this is Will," Greg said when he got to the end of the table. He lifted his shoulder slightly in Will's direction.

"It's nice to meet you, Abby," Will said, balancing his tray on one arm and reaching over to shake her hand.

Abby rose an inch out of her seat and grasped his hand quickly. "Hi," she said breathlessly. She blinked up at him, and he grinned again. *I wonder if anyone's ever kissed that dimple,* Abby thought, feeling floaty. His deep brown eyes crinkled so perfectly when he smiled.

"Uh, Ab?" Joanna said.

"Yeah?" Abby answered distractedly, still gazing up at Will.

"Where are your social skills?"

"Huh?" Abby grunted. She looked at Joanna in bewilderment. "Social skills?"

"Yeah, like, when you introduce me, your life-long friend, to Greg, your other lifelong friend?" Joanna said. "We're not talking quantum physics here, Ab."

Abby's face was on fire. She was used to Joanna's sarcastic quips, but not in front of Will and Greg. Greg was not going to let her live this down. Plus Will probably thought she was a moron now.

"Sorry," Abby said, shooting Joanna a scathing look that she hoped would hit home. Joanna seemed oblivious. She was smiling up at Greg.

"Greg Neill, this is Joanna Klein. Jo, this is Greg." Abby looked at Will, fighting for composure. "I understand you've already met my witty friend here," she joked, trying to make light of her own embarrassment.

"Yeah, I've had the pleasure," Will said without a hint of sincerity. He glanced at Joanna and then crossed in front of Greg so he could sit next to Abby.

Greg slid into the seat next to Joanna and smiled at her politely. Joanna smiled back, looking a bit more comfortable than she had a moment earlier.

Abby swallowed back the last bits of her anger over Joanna's insult. The girl was being forced to hang with a guy who had stolen her shot at stardom a couple of weeks ago. Of course she was on edge. Abby introduced Greg and Will to the rest of her friends as the guys settled into their seats.

"So, how do you guys like camp so far?" she asked when all the introductions were finished. It was a lame question, but with Joanna's current mood it seemed a lot less risky than asking Will about the acting program.

"I wasn't so sure about it at first. But now things are looking up." Greg took a swig of milk and glanced at Joanna. Abby blinked. Was Greg flirting?

"But our counselor's a freak of nature," Will said, gesturing in Damon's direction. From the amount of bones on the counselor's plate, it looked like he was munching on his sixth chicken leg. "Check it out! Is he auditioning for the next *Jurassic Park*?"

Abby laughed loudly. Will smiled at her, obviously happy that she appreciated his joke. But as her laughter subsided she noticed that Greg and Joanna were silent. In fact, they were staring at her with shocked expressions—as if she had just recited Camp Emerson's motto in Swahili.

"What?" she asked. "Do I have something on my face?" She dropped her fork with a clatter, grabbed her napkin, and wiped under her nose.

"Uh . . . no," Greg said, shooting Joanna an amused look. They both giggled a little, Greg trying unsuccessfully to hide his mirth behind his hand. Abby realized with a start that they were mocking her.

What's their problem? Abby thought. *Will's joke was funny. Well, I thought it was funny.*

"So Ab," Will began, "are you here for soccer

like Alexi Lalas over here?" Will gestured at Greg.

He called me "Ab!" Abby thought with a start.

"Give me some credit," Greg interjected. "Alexi may be a great player, but what's up with that hair? He looks like a Chia Pet on steroids."

Joanna let out a loud peal of laughter. "Oh, Greg! You're so funny!" she sang, laying a hand lightly on Greg's bare forearm.

Abby knew full well that Joanna had no clue who the world-class soccer player Will had referred to was. So she obviously didn't get Greg's joke. Abby stared at Joanna's milky white hand against Greg's tan skin and had a very strange urge to slap her friend's fingers.

Ewww. They're both *flirting! How weird!* She had hoped they'd like each other, but she'd never thought they'd *like* each other.

"To answer your question, Will," Abby said, trying to ignore the whispery conversation Greg and Joanna were conducting across the table, "I'm here for soccer. I'm gonna make varsity next year if it kills me, and the camp coach really knows how to push you to your limits."

"Cool." Will popped the last bite of his burger into his mouth. Then he actually finished chewing before he continued speaking. Was this guy for real? "I'm here because of the new acting coach. I *have* to get into Yale drama, and I figure the best way to do that is to land the lead in the play."

Joanna let out an abrupt sound that was something between a laugh and a grunt.

31

Manisha glanced over at Jo and rolled her eyes, then looked at Shira and laughed. Abby knew exactly what they were thinking—Joanna's melodrama was about to begin.

"So, Joanna, do you know what the play is gonna be?" Greg asked as he chewed on a french fry.

"Yeah, it's—"

"It's *A Match Made in Heaven*," Will interrupted, leaning forward with obvious excitement. "Which is awesome because the male lead is really meaty. It'll give me a chance to display my talent."

"Really?" Abby said, leaning her chin on her hand and blinking up at Will. "I find theater so fascinating." And she did—when Will and his perfect lips were talking about it. "Have you done a lot of acting?"

Abby felt a sudden, sharp pinch on her thigh, and she jumped out of her seat slightly, slamming her leg into the underside of the table and causing the dishes to clatter.

"Ow!" she yelped. She rubbed her thigh and stared daggers at Joanna.

"Are you okay?" Manisha asked.

"I'm fine," Abby answered. "What'd you do that for?" she snapped at Jo.

"What?" Joanna asked innocently. "Did something bite you?"

Abby felt Will's eyes dart back and forth between her and Joanna. She relaxed her shoulders. Now was not the time to deal with Jo. She could talk to her later . . . after she'd devised the proper form of punishment.

"Something like that," Abby said, giving Joanna's ankle a sharp kick as a warning. Joanna didn't flinch.

"Well, Abby, if you're really interested in theater, you should try out for the show," Will said.

Abby almost laughed at the thought of herself onstage—in front of actual people. Sure, her soccer games usually attracted a crowd, but when she was playing with her team, she was so focused, she hardly even knew the spectators were there. But the idea of a spotlight and perfect silence as all eyes trained on her . . . "I'm not exactly star material," she said finally.

"Then maybe you could sign up for stage crew. You know, you could see what goes into putting the whole thing together," Will suggested. "I'm sure the drama department would love to have you."

Abby felt her heart flutter with excitement, and she clasped her sweaty hands together under the table. This was so cool. He was practically inviting her into his life.

"That's a great idea!" she exclaimed. "Maybe I'll come by tomorrow and see if they need any help." *Maybe they need someone to be their new star's personal assistant,* she thought.

"*X-Files,* that's what this is," Joanna mumbled, tearing apart her napkin and shaking her head. "She's been kidnapped by aliens, and they've warped her brain."

Greg leaned over the table and put his hand to Abby's forehead. "She doesn't have a fever," he confirmed. "Let's get her a straitjacket." He looked at Joanna. "Does this camp have a psychiatric facility? I think we need to talk to someone about security precautions. She might start foaming at the mouth any minute."

Joanna burst out laughing. "Ab, have you ever been in a theater other than Emerson's?"

"Duh. Of course I have," Abby answered. "Am I not allowed to have new interests?" She glared at Greg. "I didn't confine you to a padded room when you took up skydiving," she protested, remembering how totally freaked she'd been when she found out Greg would be hurling himself out of an airplane.

"Hey, at least that's a sport," Greg said, biting into an apple. "Teeters fo shishies."

"Huh?" Will, Abby, and Joanna all said at the same time. Greg's ears turned red, and he swallowed. Abby knew he must have been rethinking his slurred statement.

"Theater's for um . . . actors," he said quickly. "And these two are fine actors," he continued, pointing one index finger at Joanna and the other at Will—a lame attempt at covering his butt.

Abby knew that wasn't what Greg had said, but she wasn't about to encourage Will and Joanna to argue with Greg. There was already enough tension at this table.

"Well, I for one would love to know that I had a

friend backstage for opening night," Will said. "Every great actor has supportive people behind him."

"All right, that's it," Joanna blurted, pushing her chair back with a screech. "Where do you get off?" she demanded, staring down at Will incredulously.

"Joanna . . . ," Abby began.

"No, no, it's okay, Ab," Will said, putting a hand on her shoulder. Abby felt a pleasant shiver at his touch. "Joanna obviously has something to say."

"Oh, you are just *so* mature," Joanna said through clenched teeth. Her hands gripped the edge of the table, and she looked like a wildcat ready to pounce. "I want to know what makes Mr. Cruise here think he's God's gift to our drama department. We've somehow managed to put on some incredible shows in the past without you, you know."

"Maybe we should all just calm down," Greg said, looking over his shoulder nervously. Their table had fallen silent, and Joanna had attracted Damon's attention. Kristen was looking at them with a pleading expression, a forkful of peas poised halfway between her plate and her mouth.

"Yeah, Joanna," Will said, smirking. "You're making a scene. Are you still practicing for your big soap opera break?"

Abby's stomach twisted. Okay, that was a little below the belt. Like, lower than the floor.

"Don't you ever condescend to me," Joanna said to Will. "You couldn't get a job on *Baywatch* even if you had bleached roots." She turned and stormed toward the door.

"Jo! Wait!" Abby called. She bolted up and tore after her friend, her sneakers squeaking on the linoleum floor.

Just as Joanna was about to make it outside, Kristen caught up with them. "Where do you two think you're going?" she asked. "Dinner's not over for another ten minutes."

"But Kristen—," Joanna began.

"No buts," Kristen said. Then she lowered her voice to a whisper. "C'mon, guys. Don't make me look bad on the first day. Let's go back to the table. We haven't even had announcements yet."

"Oh, fine." Joanna's shoulders slumped as Abby walked next to her through the raucous crowd back to their table.

Abby slid into her chair, and Joanna slouched down moodily next to Greg, who immediately turned his attention to her and struck up a conversation. Greg was obviously trying to cheer Jo up. Abby just hoped it would work.

"Your friend should lighten up," Will told Abby in a low voice.

"Well, that wasn't exactly cool what you said to her," Abby said quietly, fiddling with the hem of her T-shirt.

"So you know about the *Sunset Beach* thing?" Will asked, wiping his palms on his khaki shorts.

"Yeah," Abby said, looking up at him and wondering if he was planning on offering an explanation for stealing Joanna's limelight.

"I kinda feel bad about that," he said quietly. "But Abby—I'm sure you'll understand this—acting's a competitive business. You have to take advantage of every opportunity you get. I mean, if you and some stranger were told to play against each other for a shot on the varsity team, would you pull any punches?"

Abby hadn't thought of it that way. "Not a chance," she told him.

"There you go," Will said, finishing off his water. "I gotta do what I can, you know?"

Abby nodded, feeling slightly disloyal to Joanna. But Joanna would've probably done the same thing to Will if she'd been big enough to block *him* out of the shot. Abby knew she was pretty ruthless when it came to auditions.

She smiled and let the tension fall away from her shoulders. Maybe she could talk to Joanna later and remind her of that. Maybe, just maybe, Jo would be reasonable and give Will another chance.

"So, what exactly is *A Match Made in Heaven* about?"

"It's about this guy who matches up his brother with this woman," Will explained, his eyes lighting up at the subject. "And once that works out, he thinks he has a talent for it, so he starts matching up everyone in town. . . ."

Abby watched his mouth as he spoke and let her mind drift a little. So far, she knew that Will was driven, had a quick—if slightly evil—sense of

37

humor, had perfect table manners, and was not at all bad to look at. All of this added up to a very interesting package.

Suddenly Joanna laughed again, and Abby looked over to see her friend leaning almost her entire upper body on Greg's arm.

Abby smiled wanly. It was a little strange watching her two best friends flirt. But if they got together and she and Will got together, it might be kind of cool. They could have the first summer-long double date in history.

Babs stood up at the front of the room and called the mess hall to attention. As the room started to quiet down, Abby leaned back in her chair, waiting for the familiar words of the camp director's overused opening speech to fill her ears. It was great to be back.

"Welcome, campers, to the most exciting experience of your life. . . ."

Abby smiled and looked around at her friends. *Let the games begin!*

Four

GREG GULPED THE Gatorade from his flimsy plastic cup like he hadn't seen liquid in a month.

"Ugh! What a workout!" Abby exclaimed as she flopped down on the metal bench beside him.

It was Monday morning, and they'd just finished their first grueling soccer practice. Abby pulled a white elastic out of her hair and let her brown locks fall around her rosy cheeks. Greg smiled. Even though Abby was just a friend, he always noticed how pretty she looked after some serious exercise. Her skin glowed, and her blue eyes were bright with excitement over a scrimmage well played.

"You look great, Ab," Greg told her. He tilted his head back and shook the cup over his mouth, hoping for one last drop. He didn't get it.

"You're a lousy liar, Neill. How could I look great when I feel like a dying jellyfish?" she asked, laughing.

"Yeah, well, you should have seen *me* when that stupid bugle woke me up this morning." Greg shuddered, remembering how the annoyingly loud sound had abruptly interrupted his sleep. "I looked like death warmed over."

"It's called reveille, loser," Abby said.

"Whatever. All I know is that the bugle boy must die."

Abby giggled. She flipped her hair over and twisted it into a big puffy bun at the top of her head. Sitting back up, she batted her eyelashes at Greg and patted her new hairdo.

"Now how do I look?" she asked, fanning herself primly with her hand.

"Ridiculous," Greg answered. He crushed his cup and hurled it into a nearby garbage can with a perfect hook shot. "Two points!" he said.

"Great job out there today, guys." Logan Thomas, their soccer instructor, was smiling down at them. Logan coached soccer at the local high school, and his team had been the Pennsylvania state champs for five years in a row—ever since Logan had started coaching there. He was twenty-eight years old, but he had a mop of curly red hair and a face full of freckles that made him look like he was still a young Boy Scout.

"It's cool that you let the guys and girls practice together, Logan," Greg said.

"I think it helps to mix it up," Logan explained. "Everyone has a different style of playing, and you can all learn from each other."

"We should have a mixed league," Abby said thoughtfully. "Maybe we could start our own team back home."

"I wish I had you two on *my* team," Logan said. He crouched down to search for something under a chair, and his calf muscles bulged noticeably. Now *that* was a soccer player's physique. Then Logan stood up, holding a large bottle of water. "Do you play varsity at home, Greg?" he asked.

Greg smiled, flattered that Logan thought he was talented enough to play varsity. "Nah, not yet," Greg answered, leaning over to pull his shin guards out of his socks. "But I did see more playing time than any other freshman on JV."

"I don't doubt it." Logan looked at Abby. "If you both work hard this summer, you're going to have a real shot at lettering next year. Right, Stewart?"

"Right, Coach." Abby nodded happily. Her bun bounced around like a little punching bag. Greg chuckled.

"Let's get going, you guys," Kristen said, jogging up behind Logan, a group of campers following. "We gotta get down to lunch."

"Can we have a few minutes?" Abby asked, leaning her head back and stretching her arms. "I don't want to move yet."

Kristen looked at Logan, and he shrugged. "I guess it's okay," Kristen said. "Just don't be too long."

"Thanks," Greg responded.

"Later, guys," Logan said, shouldering his bag. "I expect to see you two at tonight's counselors versus campers relay races. Prepare to be destroyed." Abby and Greg both laughed at his mock-scary tone. "Have fun at your afternoon activity," he added, then walked down the hill with Kristen and the group of campers toward the mess hall.

"Hey, yeah. I haven't signed up for a minor yet," Greg said.

"You can do it after lunch." Abby's voice sounded flat. Her eyes were riveted on her cleats, and her forehead was all scrunched up as if she were contemplating the meaning of life.

"What's the matter, ugly?" he asked.

"What if he's wrong?" Abby returned, lifting her face. Her expression was so pained, it made Greg's heart flop.

"About what?"

"What if I don't make varsity this year? What if I *never* make varsity?"

Greg laughed. "You're kidding, right?"

"It's not funny!" Abby protested, slapping him on the arm.

Greg straightened up and tried to keep himself from smiling, but he couldn't. Abby *never* make varsity? That was like saying there'd never be another Bond movie. It was just an inevitable event.

"Abby, you would've been playing varsity last year if it wasn't for that stupid league rule, and you know it," Greg said, watching as Simon and

Dominic struggled with the huge bags full of soccer balls and headed off the field. Greg caught Dom's eye and waved. Dom nodded back. They'd all played poker last night with M&M's instead of chips, and Greg had taken Simon, Will, and Dominic for all they were worth. They were going to be good guys to have around—especially if Greg wanted snack food.

"Yeah, maybe," Abby said quietly, bringing him back to the conversation. She kicked at the white sideline stripe with the toe of her black cleat, causing little white tufts of powder to float into the air. "What's up with that rule, anyway? Freshmen can't play varsity, and seniors can't play JV. What if, like, the next Pelé was a freshman, and you'd be guaranteed the championship? Or what if some senior totally blew but just wanted to play? She'd sit on the varsity bench all season. What's up with that?"

Abby's whole body slumped. She was always able to torture herself over nonissues if she got in the right—or wrong—frame of mind.

"It's never gonna happen to you, Ab, so why get all upset over it?" Greg asked, standing and grabbing his soccer ball. He stood in front of her and started to juggle with his feet. "Besides, you have the whole summer to get into primo shape. Coach Citron will be begging you to play starting forward when we get back."

"You're right," Abby said, following his soccer ball with her eyes as he juggled. "I just have to spend all my energy this summer on soccer. I can't let myself get distracted."

Greg popped the ball up to shoulder height and caught it in his hands. "Well, it's too late for that. I'd say you're already plenty distracted."

"What do you mean?" Abby asked, standing up. She bent and touched her toes, letting out a little groan as her muscles stretched.

"Oh, *Will!* You're so *funny*," Greg teased in a high-pitched voice. "Oh, *please* let me join the drama department so I can follow you around all summer and carry your huge ego for you!"

"Greg! I didn't sound like that!" Abby protested, her head popping up. She looked unusually pale. "I've never sounded like that in my life."

Greg dropped his soccer ball and stopped it with his foot. "Oh, *Will!*" He pretended to flip long hair off his shoulder. "Tell that *Jurassic Park* joke again. It was just *so* funny. Can I clear your dishes for you?"

Abby let out a snort of laughter at Greg's performance but quickly turned her expression serious.

"All right! That's it!" She lunged forward and kicked the ball out from under Greg's foot, causing him to temporarily lose his balance. When he looked up, she was already halfway down the field, dribbling in front of her. "I did *not* offer to clear his dishes, *loser!*" Abby yelled over her shoulder.

Greg laughed and took off after her.

"C'mon, Greg!" she called. "Can't you catch up with the flirty girly-girl? Maybe you should just give up soccer and join the *cheerleading squad* when we get back home. I hear they're looking for new blood."

Oh, man, low blow, Greg thought, upping his speed. He came up behind her, but she blocked him, using some fancy footwork to maneuver the ball away from him. Finally Greg got frustrated and hooked her ankle with his, sending them both sprawling on the ground. The ball bounced and rolled slowly away, stopping about two feet from the goal.

"Foul!" Abby yelled with a grin, propping herself up on her elbows. Her bun had fallen, and half of her mop of hair was covering her face.

Greg smiled back at her. "No, that cheerleading comment was foul," he said. "You are never going to let me forget that, are you?"

Early this past school year Greg had lost a dare with some older guys and had been forced to wear a cheerleading uniform to school on the day before a football game—the day all the cheerleaders wore their outfits to school. He'd been called into the principal's office and was sent home to change within fifteen minutes of walking through the front doors, but most of the student body had already gotten a glimpse of him in the lobby. Greg knew that nobody had been more amused than Abby.

"It was so classic," she said, standing up and brushing the grass off her heather gray cotton shorts. "I'll never forget when Joey Britten held your skirt in the air in front of the home ec room."

Greg laughed. In retrospect it *was* pretty funny.

She offered him her hand. "C'mon, we have to go to lunch."

Greg clutched her forearm and pulled himself up. Glancing around, he noticed that they were the only campers left on the field.

"And I still say that was a foul," Abby said, poking him in the chest. Her blue eyes were sparkling, and she skipped a little as she headed off the field in front of him.

"I'm glad to see you're in a good mood again," Greg said. He placed his hands on her shoulders and kneaded her muscles with his thumbs.

"Yeah, well, beating your sorry butt always makes me feel better."

"Hey! You did *not* beat me—"

"Whatever." Abby waved a hand dismissively as they headed down the trail. She looked at Greg thoughtfully for a moment. "Did I really look like that much of an idiot at dinner last night?" She pulled back her hair again and fastened it into a low ponytail. Greg realized that although Abby always maintained that she didn't care about her appearance, she played with her hair an awful lot.

"You weren't *that* bad," Greg answered. "But you were kind of all over him. I've never seen you act like that before, Ab. It was, like, freaking me out." Greg shuddered a little for effect.

"Ugh! I was just trying to get to *know* the guy," Abby said indignantly. "What's wrong with that?" She kicked a rock and sent it shooting into a wild raspberry bush.

"Nothing!" Greg threw his hands up in surrender. "I just don't want to see you get mixed up with the wrong guy. Joanna told me that—"

"Oh! Now you and Jo are talking about me behind my back?" Abby asked, stopping short. She faced him, crossing her arms in front of her chest. "I get it! You guys thought you had cornered the market on shameless flirting?"

Greg felt his ears turning red. He suddenly wished he were wearing a wool cap, even though it was almost ninety degrees out. "Aha!" Abby reached out and wiggled his earlobe between two fingers. "I *knew* you liked her!"

Even though Greg was famous for his ability to keep a straight face and remain calm under pressure, his ears always betrayed him. They were worse than Pinocchio's nose.

"Well, what's not to like?" Greg asked, maneuvering around her and continuing down the hill. "She's totally hot, and . . . and . . . she has a good sense of humor."

"Why? Because she laughed at *your* jokes?" Abby laughed, falling into step beside him. "I dunno, Greg; if you think you can handle her . . . ," she said nonchalantly.

"What's that supposed to mean?" Greg demanded. His foot slid on a loose rock and his leg shot out from under him. Greg grabbed Abby for balance, and she steadied him easily.

"Whoa, there, lover boy," she joked.

"Why don't you think I can handle Joanna?"

Greg asked, straightening himself up. "What is she, a closet psycho or something?"

"No. Not technically," Abby answered. "But you saw her little performance at dinner last night. I've told you before, she's a total drama queen. The girl overreacts to everything. Sometimes I think she's gonna bust a blood vessel if the ratio of ice to soda in her glass is off. I mean, I love her for her psychoticness, but it might be hard for a boyfriend to handle."

"High maintenance?" Greg asked.

"More like premium," Abby amended. "Don't get me wrong," she continued as they reached the clearing at the bottom of the hill. "I think both of you guys are great. And having my two best friends couple up might be cool. I just don't know if a wuss boy like you . . ." She looked at him coyly.

"Oh, first I'm a cheerleader, and now I'm a wuss boy?" Greg asked. "I'll give you five, Stewart. And you'd better hope I don't catch you this time," he challenged.

"I don't need five. See ya!" Abby said, just before taking off at a sprint.

"One . . . two . . . five!" Greg yelled. He tore off after Abby, the wind whipping his bangs back from his face and carrying the sound of Abby's laughter to his ears.

He closed the gap between them and was about to reach for Abby's wrist when he was startled by the shrill clang of a large bell.

They both skidded to a stop and stared at each other, petrified.

"Lunch!" they yelled in unison. Greg was off in a heartbeat with Abby by his side. He was dreading what Damon might come up with as punishment this time. Sitting with the girls had turned out fine, but who knew what else Damon could conjure up? Greg would probably end up spit shining the guy's barbells for the rest of the summer.

As they neared Lake Emerson, Greg caught sight of the mess hall and was grateful to see that campers were still making their way inside.

"Wait!" Abby gasped, grabbing his arm as they jogged up the steps and through the door. "I just got an idea."

Greg's eyes darted to their table as Abby paused for a moment to catch her breath. Joanna and Will were turned in completely opposite directions. Joanna was chatting animatedly with Shira, and Will was twisted around toward the table beside theirs, laughing along with Damon and Simon.

"What's up?" Greg asked her.

"It's about those two," Abby answered, raising her chin in the direction of Joanna and Will.

"What about 'em?"

"Well, I know Jo better than anyone, and you live with Will. . . ." Abby's voice trailed off. She looked at Greg suggestively.

Greg was about to ask her what she was talking about when all of a sudden it dawned on him. "I help you get yours, and you help me get mine, right?"

"Exactly. We could—"

"You two lovebirds planning on joining us anytime soon?" Kristen's voice boomed across the noisy dining room. Half the people in the mess hall turned to gape at them.

"Love, uh, birds?" Abby stammered.

There go the ears, Greg thought. He grabbed Abby's wrist, ducked his head slightly, and pulled her toward their table. As they got closer Joanna looked Greg in the eye and graced him with a heart-stopping smile. His uneasiness melted away.

At least she knows Abby and I aren't together. That's all that matters, Greg thought, sliding into his seat next to Joanna.

He shot Abby a reassuring smile. She looked surprised for a second, then seemed to realize his meaning and smiled back. She greeted Joanna, took her seat next to Will, and immediately turned her attention to him.

Greg grinned happily as Joanna passed him a tray of sandwiches. With a force like him and Abby teaming up against Joanna and Will, all of them were bound to be coupled off before long.

Five

"*D*ON'T TOUCH ANYTHING!" Abby stage-whispered, slapping the back of Greg's hand.

"Calm down, woman," Greg said, pulling his hand back like a cat with a wounded paw. "What's the point of being here if we can't have any fun?"

Abby looked around the musty lighting booth of the small theater. She and Greg were putting the first phase of their love plot into action. After lunch she had convinced him to join stage crew for their minor, hoping to guarantee themselves extra hours of match-making time with the objects of their affection. But the director, Ms. Marshall, had assigned them to lighting, which put them in the back of the theater, above the balcony seats—as far from the stage as you could possibly get without leaving the building. She'd told them to come up here and wait for her to join them so she could explain how everything worked.

"This reeks," Abby said, climbing onto a tall

stool and pushing up the sleeves of her red Cornell sweatshirt. "How are we ever going to get their attention if we're stuck up here the whole time?"

"Hey! Check this out! Why do you think there's a microphone up here?" Greg held out an old-fashioned microphone—the kind with a big silver ball and a really long, thick black cord. "D'ya think it's plugged in?" he asked, flashing a mischievous grin.

"Greg, don't mess with that!" Abby said, laughing in spite of herself. Greg could be so silly when he was hyper. His energy was infectious.

"Ladies and gentlemen!" Greg put on a sports announcer's voice and spoke into the microphone. "Here she is, the most valuable player of this year's Olympic soccer team. Four-time gold medalist, the great number three—Abby Stewart. Give it up!" Greg faked the sound of a roaring crowd and pulled Abby off her seat by the wrist. She played along, giving a deep bow and waving to the "crowd."

"Could this place be any cooler?" Greg remarked, placing the microphone on a low table. "Look at all these switches and buttons and crazy levers. It's like the *Millennium Falcon* up here. Or the space shuttle." He picked up the mike again. "Houston, we have a problem," he said, cupping the mike with his hand.

Abby put her hand in front of her mouth as if she were holding a walkie-talkie. "This is Houston. We read you. Who *is* this, and what are you doing on this frequency?"

"This is Han Solo," Greg answered, grinning.

"I can't believe you don't know who I am. I've only saved the rebellion's butt, like, a hundred times. Don't make me mad, Houston."

Abby tried to contain her laughter, wondering if she was the only person on the planet who loved Greg's stupid sense of humor so much. He was so great to have around. Back on the soccer field he'd known exactly what to do to cheer her up. And now he was making this boring job fun.

"Will Stevenson?" Abby's head popped up when she heard Ms. Marshall call Will's name. The director was holding auditions down below.

Abby peeked out the large plate glass window at the black plank stage. Will was walking to the center of the stage. He was wearing a black T-shirt and a pair of denim shorts, and his hair hung loosely around his shoulders. He looked like one of those models from the Polo Jeans ads—or an MTV vee-jay. Abby crossed her fingers and tried to mentally project him a message of good luck.

"He looks like a girl!" Greg said, jostling into position next to her.

"Shhh!"

"I'm sorry, but the dude needs to spend some quality time with a good barber," Greg commented.

Abby rolled her eyes.

"You can begin," Ms. Marshall said.

Will started to recite his monologue, moving about the stage, his voice projecting throughout the theater. Abby shivered with delight. He was really

53

good—he looked so natural up there onstage.

"I wonder what this does," Greg said, flicking a switch. The stage was instantly bathed in pink light. Will didn't flinch, but Ms. Marshall turned in her seat and looked up at them.

"Quit it!" Abby hissed, flipping the switch to off. "You're distracting her!"

Greg leaned over the switchboard. "Hmmm . . . maybe I'll try these little red switches," he said in a playfully challenging voice, poising his hand over a row of round buttons.

"Don't you dare," Abby protested, jumping up and grabbing his wrist. She twisted his arm behind him and held it against his back. Greg laughed, and Abby felt her mouth start to twitch, but she tried to sound serious. "If you mess up his audition, I will so kill you."

"Oh, yeah?" Greg reached with his other arm and grabbed her side at her most ticklish spot. Abby yelped and released his arm. Greg twisted around and lunged for the switchboard. Abby grabbed his shirt. She pulled with all her might while Greg leaned forward, stretching his arms out toward the switches. Finally the fabric slipped from her fingers, and Greg shot forward.

"Greg!" In desperation Abby jumped on his back, wrapping her legs around his waist and laughing the entire time. "Quit it!" she cried, trying to quiet her giggles.

"Hey! Get off me!" Greg said, grabbing at her behind him awkwardly. They stumbled backward, and Abby almost slammed into the wall until Greg shifted his weight and they hurtled forward.

"Oooh, Greg—watch out!" Abby clung to Greg, afraid he was going to lose his balance and send her tumbling to the splintery wooden floor of the booth. Suddenly Greg's foot caught on the leg of the stool and he spun around and buckled, flinging Abby down on her backside . . . right on top of the switchboard.

There was a bright flash of light, and Abby heard someone yell. She turned to look out the window just as Will threw his arms up in front of his face—and walked right off the stage, falling to the ground with a loud thud.

Abby's stomach turned. "Oh, my gosh. We blinded him."

"Well," Greg said, leaning one arm on the switchboard and smiling. "*That* got his attention."

Abby practically flew down the thinly carpeted steps into the main seating area of the auditorium. As Greg followed he bit the inside of his cheek to keep himself from laughing. He would never forget the image of Will falling off the edge of the stage. It was classic—straight out of a Monty Python movie.

By the time they made it to the front row, Ms. Marshall and some other campers had helped Will out of the orchestra pit and over to a seat. He was running his fingers through his hair and telling everyone around him that he was fine. But even from the side of the room Greg could tell that Will's face was beet red, and he was sweating buckets. Greg covered his smile with his hand.

Abby fell to her knees in front of Will. "Are you all right?" she asked, looking up into his face. "Are you hurt? Where does it hurt?"

Greg's face fell. Who *was* that girl in Abby's body anyway? She was being so melodramatic. He watched as she took Will's hand in hers and stared into his face with concern. Very Florence Nightingale. A couple of months ago, when Greg had fallen out of their old climbing tree, Abby had simply asked if he was okay and then told him to get up and stop being a wimp.

Maybe she just knows that Will is more fragile than I am, Greg thought, absently tightening his arm muscles.

Then he saw her reach up and tenderly touch Will's forehead. Greg winced. *Ugh! She like,* touched *him!*

"Are you responsible for this?"

Greg's shoulders tensed at the stern sound of the voice behind him. He turned slowly, expecting to find Babs standing there, ready to slap him with ten demerits and relegate him to kitchen duty for the rest of the summer. Instead he was staring into Joanna's laughing blue eyes. He relaxed.

Joanna really was beautiful. Abby's Nurse Hathaway performance was immediately forgotten.

"I don't want to brag or anything," he said, buffing his knuckles against his cotton shirt.

Joanna laughed and reached up to pat Greg's shoulder. "You should be proud," she told him. "That spotlight was a total stroke of genius. I'm just sorry I didn't think of it myself."

Greg smiled and settled into one of the auditorium seats. Joanna followed suit, perching herself on the edge of a chair and crossing her legs at the knee. Greg couldn't help noticing that Joanna was once again wearing very short shorts. He looked up at her face quickly, hoping to stop his ears before they started to get red.

"I wish I could say we did it on purpose," he said with a laugh. "But Abby and I were . . . um . . . having a little disagreement over who should man the controls, and, well, Will was just an innocent victim."

"Still, you might have done me a tremendous favor," Joanna said, leaning toward him slightly. A shock of red hair fell over her right eye, and she made no move to brush it away. The effect was incredibly sexy.

Greg squirmed in his seat slightly. "How's that?" he asked.

"Do you really think they're gonna give the starring role to a guy who can't even figure out where the stage ends? He'll probably be relegated to the chorus, and I'll get to work with someone who can actually fit his head through the door." Joanna moved back in her seat and crossed her arms behind her head. "Isn't life blissful?"

Greg sat up with a start. "You think Ms. Marshall might count this against him?" he asked, alarmed. He hadn't thought that they'd ruined Will's entire summer. He didn't hate the guy *that* much. In fact, he didn't really hate the guy at all. Greg glanced over at Will.

I just wish he would stop looking at Abby as if she were God's gift to lousy actors, he thought uncomfortably. But still, if someone told Greg he couldn't play soccer all summer, he'd be on the next bus back to Passmore before you could say "sidelined."

"It wasn't his fault," Greg protested.

"So?" Joanna asked, sitting up again. She reached over and laid her hand over Greg's. A sharp tingle ran up his arm. "The point is, I'm very grateful." She fluttered her eyelashes at him, and Greg's heart pounded. She was practically throwing herself at his feet.

Greg's eyes shot over Joanna's shoulder, and he saw that Abby was now sitting next to Will, and they were talking and laughing easily. She caught his eye and flashed him a thumbs-up sign.

Greg smiled and focused back on Joanna, who was staring up at the stage. "How grateful would you be, exactly?" he asked flirtatiously.

"Joanna Klein?" Ms. Marshall's voice rang out suddenly.

Joanna bolted up. "I guess they're starting again," she said, pulling down on the hem of her little black shorts. She looked down at Greg. "Why don't we talk about this more later?" she proposed. Then she strutted up the stage steps.

Greg watched in admiration as Joanna launched into her monologue.

Yes, he definitely *did* want to talk about this later.

Six

GREG ROLLED HIS shoulders and swung his head back and forth, trying to stretch out his neck. Then he bounced up and down on the balls of his feet, looking over the shoulders of the players in line in front of him. Five more people before it was his turn to take another shot at the net.

Relax, it's no big deal, he told himself.

Greg hated drills—he was more of a team player than the type who enjoyed being singled out. Having everyone's critical eyes on him at the same time was not his idea of fun. So far they'd each taken two shots at the goal, and Greg's first attempt had been blocked easily by Simon, who was playing goalie. The second had whizzed over the net, clearing the top of the goal by two feet. Everyone had started chanting "air ball" until Logan had told them to cool it and concentrate on their own shots.

"Where are you, Ab?" Greg muttered, tilting his

head back and looking up at the cloudless blue sky.

"Hi!" Abby scooted into line in front of Greg and grabbed both of his arms. "I have great news!"

"Where've you been?" Greg asked irritably as Abby released him.

"What's the matter?" she asked. "Have you been tanking your shots?"

"No . . . well, yes. And thanks for rubbing my face in it. How did you know anyway?" he asked.

"You only get all touchy when you've been stinking," Abby said, whirling around to face the net. Her ponytail whipped Greg in the chest. "Don't worry. Now that I'm here, you'll be fine."

"How do you figure?" Greg asked as the guy in front of Abby ran forward, charging the goal. He faked right and then shot left, but the goalie saw it coming and dove to catch the ball.

"I'm your good-luck charm," she said, winking at him over her shoulder.

"You're up, Stewart!" Logan yelled, holding his clipboard against his chest over by the sideline.

Abby stood still for a moment and then charged the ball in front of her. She caught it with her feet, dribbled forward, and shot with a powerful kick. The ball flew just high of the goalie's outstretched fingers and rocketed into the back of the orange net.

"Nice one," Logan said, making a note on his pad.

Some good-luck charm, Greg thought. *She's just gonna make me look even worse.*

Greg ran forward and, rather than dribbling the ball toward the box, decided to go with the element of surprise. He caught the ball with the inside of his foot and shot toward the far right corner. For an agonizing moment he thought he'd shot wide again, but the ball mercifully hit the post and ricocheted behind Simon into the net.

"Yes!" Greg called out, throwing his fist in the air and then pulling it down to pump it by his side. He ran back to the end of the line and joined Abby, who held up her hand for a high five.

"See? Told ya!" she said happily.

"Wish you'd shown up sooner," Greg said, grabbing her ponytail and flinging it up so that it fell over her face.

Abby swung her hair out of her eyes. "But I had a good reason for being late!" she exclaimed. "You know how we were wondering whether we should sign up for a new minor after what happened on Monday?"

Greg nodded. They'd had a day to think about it because they'd had a free period instead of their minor yesterday afternoon.

"Well, Ms. Marshall grabbed me on my way out of the bathroom after breakfast and guess what—we've been fired! Isn't that great?" Abby hopped up and down, grinning up at Greg.

"How is that great? Doesn't that just totally kill phase one?" Greg asked, keeping his voice down so none of the other players could hear him. They might ask what phase one was all about, and he really didn't want to try to explain the whole love plot thing.

"Let me finish!" Abby slapped her hand over Greg's mouth. Greg's eyes widened. Abby was

61

obviously losing her mind. "We've been reassigned to sets!" she cried. "Isn't that fabulous? Well, isn't it?"

Greg didn't answer. He couldn't. So he opened his mouth and licked her hand.

Abby recoiled and wiped her hand on Greg's soccer jersey. "Jeez! Grow up already!" She laughed.

"Well, how was I supposed to answer you while you were suffocating me?" he asked as they moved forward in the line. "Sets, huh? Maybe we could create another marshmallow masterpiece."

Abby laughed again. "That was the best piece of scenery on the whole stage," she said indignantly.

"Stewart! We're waiting!"

Greg looked up. They'd already gotten to the front of the line without noticing.

"Sorry!" Abby called. She ran forward and executed her shot easily.

Greg smiled, remembering their eighth-grade production of *A Midsummer Night's Dream*. He and Abby had spent two months working on one tree that ended up looking like a green marshmallow on a stick.

Once Abby had run back to the end of the line, Greg dribbled the ball up and faked out Simon, lobbing the ball easily over the goalie's head. Then he jogged back and joined Abby.

"So what if we're not artistic?" she asked. "At least we'll be at stage level, so we'll get to hang out with Joanna and Will instead of being relegated to the tower."

"Good point," Greg said, watching as Dominic

took a shot. "Thank God Will got the lead even though he took that nosedive. I don't even want to know what it would've been like to live with him if we'd screwed up his audition."

"Seriously," Abby agreed. "I thought I was gonna die when he fell off that stage. I can't believe he doesn't hate me."

"How could anyone hate you, Ab?" Greg said, smiling. "You're, like, the sweetest person on the planet."

Abby grinned. "And the smartest!" she added. "I've come up with phase two!"

"All right, everyone!" Logan called. "Get over here and grab a drink. I'm gonna split you up into scrimmage teams."

"What's phase two?" Greg asked as they jogged over to the sideline. "Are we gonna push *Joanna* off the stage now?"

"No, stupid—although I'd like to at this point. She's acting so bizarre this summer. I mean, she got the lead, but instead of focusing on that and being happy, she's all upset because she has to work with Will." Abby grabbed two cups and held one under the barrel-size jug of water while Greg threw the little tap switch.

"It's too bad they don't get along," Greg said. "That would make life much easier."

"Definitely," Abby said, holding up a cup for Greg. "But anyway, phase two is a double date."

"How do you date at camp?" Greg asked. "Won't Damon's counselor alarm go off if we're not in our bunks by nine?"

"Dates don't have to be in the evening," Abby chided. "We have a free period on Thursday mornings, right? And tomorrow's Thursday, so I thought maybe we could all go for a hike or something."

"Hey, yeah!" Greg said. "Damon told me they have some great trails on the grounds."

"Right. So I thought if you invited Will and I invited Joanna—," Abby explained, crushing her cup and tossing it back and forth from hand to hand.

"Then it won't *look* like a date," Greg finished. But suddenly he got a queasy feeling in his stomach. "But Joanna and Will hate each other," he said. "Do you really think they'll agree to go?"

"Joanna's my best friend," Abby told him. "I'll just play the guilt card over the way she slammed me at lunch the other day and tell her she has to come. Maybe if they're forced to spend some more time together, they'll see that they're not totally repulsive and call a truce. Besides, why would she pass up a chance to hang out with you?"

"No girl in her right mind would pass that up," Greg agreed. "But what about Will?"

"Are you saying he won't want to spend time with me?" Abby asked, glaring at Greg playfully.

"I'm sorry," Greg responded, backing up. "I just lost my logic for a second there."

"Abby! Greg!" Logan interrupted. "You guys are on blue. Let's get going."

He handed them each a blue vest, which they pulled on over their shirts. Then Logan blew his whistle.

"So we're all set with phase two?" Abby asked,

dropping to the ground to tighten her laces.

"Aye, aye, Captain," Greg said with a smile.

He jogged behind Abby out to center field. *I should always have Abby plan my dates,* he thought. *She knows exactly what she's doing.*

"Ow! Greg! How much farther are we going?" Joanna asked. "I just got bitten for, like, the fiftieth time."

"I *told* you to put on some of that bug spray," Abby called over her shoulder without slowing down. "And we've only been hiking for ten minutes."

"Are you kidding?" Joanna asked. "Greg, tell me she's kidding."

Abby turned around as Joanna sat down on a rock and Greg squatted in front of her. "C'mon, Joanna," he said gently. "This trail is pretty easy. And when we get to the top, the view will make it all worth it."

"Promise?" Joanna asked.

"Promise," Greg confirmed with a smile.

Abby felt like she was gonna hurl. Joanna was acting like a total wimp, and Greg was coddling her like a baby. Why had she never noticed before how irritating Joanna's whiny side could be?

"What's her deal?" Will asked, coming up alongside Abby. He stepped into a small hole and lost his balance for a moment, then grabbed a branch to steady himself.

"You okay?" Abby asked.

"Yeah, I'm fine," Will said. "I guess I'm just used to walking on flat asphalt."

"Maybe Joanna is missing the city too." Abby shrugged. "She's not exactly Iron Man. Come to think of it, I don't think I've ever seen her voluntarily participate in a sport. She usually only does what she has to. Maybe she really does like Greg."

"Joanna's here because of Greg?" Will asked, looking at the two of them, who were talking in low tones a few yards behind.

Abby felt her cheeks fire up. She hadn't meant to let that information slip. But then, she couldn't think of a reason not to tell Will about Greg's crush. What difference would it make? She decided to play it down just in case.

"I don't know. I just sort of think they make a good couple," Abby told him. She looked up at Will's profile. His neck was so close, she could see the little stubbly hairs under his chin.

"Whatever," Will said, sounding irritated. "Are you guys ready to go or what?" he called back.

Joanna glared at Will for a moment, narrowing her eyes into little slits. "We're ready," she said finally.

Greg stood and held out his arms to Joanna. She grabbed his hands and hoisted herself up. Abby watched as Joanna "tripped" and fell into Greg's arms with a giggle. Will turned abruptly and forged ahead on the trail. Abby's stomach turned again. Joanna could teach a college course in flirting. And Greg seemed to be eating it up. Couldn't he see the fakeness factor?

Joanna started walking at a fast clip. She blew by Abby and kept walking until she was ahead of Will. Greg caught up with Abby, detached her water bottle from her backpack, and squirted a generous amount into his mouth. Then he handed it back to her.

"She wants me," he said. He took off after Joanna and Will.

Abby rolled her eyes and reattached her bottle to the little black strap. "At least he's happy," she said. "I might as well be a gnat where Will's concerned." She noticed that they all had stopped up ahead. Joanna and Greg were discussing something while Will studiously snapped a small twig into even smaller pieces.

Abby walked up behind them and put a hand on Greg's back. "What's the matter?" she asked, looking down the trail.

"It's dark down there," Joanna whined. "Do you guys know where you're going?"

"It's only dark down there because there're more trees," Will said, coming up beside them.

"I just don't feel like getting lost, okay?" Joanna said.

"What's that for?" Greg asked, pointing to the large branch Will was holding.

"Walking stick," Will said, holding it out with a proud smile.

"Ah," Greg said. He shot Abby an amused glance. Abby knew exactly what Greg was thinking—*Will's a real mountain man now.*

"C'mon, you guys! We're wasting time!" Abby said, breaking between Joanna and Greg and starting down the trail toward the heavily shaded area. Her steps quickened down the slight slope, and then she found herself at the bottom. Greg followed her, but they both stopped when they realized the others weren't moving.

Abby turned around with an exasperated sigh. Joanna was standing at the top of the little dip in the trail, her arms crossed in front of her pink T-shirt, her chin lifted defiantly.

"Don't worry, Joanna," Greg said solicitously. "The trail's marked. We won't get lost."

"Promise?" Joanna said, a lost puppy dog look in her blue eyes.

"Promise," Greg said, smiling sweetly.

Abby waited for him to roll his eyes at her. He didn't. What was all this "promise" insanity about anyway? They sounded like one of those annoying couples who rub noses and talk baby talk in the school cafeteria.

Joanna glanced at Will. "Ladies first," he said, bowing slightly.

"Don't do me any favors," Joanna told him. Then she started down the slope very slowly, picking her way gingerly around the rocks. Will came after her, brandishing his walking stick with pride.

Just as Jo got to the bottom of the slope, Will put his walking stick down right on his foot. Abby watched in horror as if witnessing a car crash in slow motion. The sharp tip of the waking stick caught in the looped lace of Will's hiking boot, and Will tripped and tumbled forward. His eyes flew open in surprise, and he reached out to grab the only figure within his grasp—Joanna.

"Hey! What're you—" Joanna's yelp of surprise was cut off as she and Will hurtled forward and landed with a thud at Abby and Greg's feet. They didn't move for a moment, and Abby stared at their entwined forms. They looked like a Twister game gone ridiculously wrong.

"Um . . . are you guys okay?" Greg asked.

"Get *off* me, you klutz!" Joanna shrieked, freeing herself from under Will's legs and struggling to stand up. "Ugh!" she groaned, looking down at her clothes. "Look at me!" Her outfit was covered with dirt, and she had a small cut below her left knee.

Will stood up. "It . . . it was an accident," he stammered. "It's not like I meant to trip."

"Aren't you even going to apologize?" Joanna asked.

Will shrugged. "Sorry."

Joanna looked like she was going to explode. "This hike is *so* over!" She turned on her heel and started to stalk away. Then she stopped abruptly. "Greg. Are you coming?" she asked.

Abby looked at Greg. His mouth was hanging open, reflecting the same shock Abby felt over the scene that had just played out before them. "I . . . I . . ."

"Fine! Forget it," Joanna said. In a moment she'd ascended the little slope and disappeared over the other side.

"I'm gonna go get cleaned up," Will said, brushing his hands down the front of his dirty white polo shirt. "I think I'm pretty dangerous to have around." He shot a strained smile at Abby and then took off after Joanna.

"Wait!" Abby called when she finally found her voice. "I—"

"I think it's too late," Greg said. "It's time to admit that a hike wasn't the best idea we've ever come up with."

"That's a major news flash," Abby said with a tight laugh. "Maybe we should go after them."

"Nah," Greg said. "Let's give them some time to calm down. We can apologize later. I don't think Joanna's functioning in the realm of reality right now."

"Oh, so you did notice," Abby said. "I thought I was losing my mind."

"They just weren't cut out to keep up with us," Greg teased. "Speaking of which, you ready to take on this mountain for real?"

Abby squared her shoulders and smiled at Greg. "Race ya!" she said.

Greg grinned and bolted, scrambling down the trail.

"Hey! I didn't say you could have a head start!" Abby cried, running after him.

"Sore loser!" Greg called.

As Abby caught up with him she realized she was kind of glad that Jo and Will were gone. She'd been self-conscious around Will, which took away from the whole point of a hike—relaxation. And watching Joanna and Greg had been beyond irritating. At least now she and Greg were alone and having fun . . . even if they had probably just lost their chances for love this summer.

Seven

"**G**O, ABBY!" GREG yelled at the top of his lungs. The small crowd that had gathered on the sidelines was making a lot of noise, and Greg wanted to be sure Abby could hear him over the rest of the cheers. It was Friday morning, and Emerson was playing in its first intercamp match.

Abby was playing an amazing game. It was stunning—unbelievable. And Greg felt as if he were out on the field with her. Her adrenaline and excitement were coursing through *his* veins. It was the coolest thing.

Greg's heart pounded in his chest, partially from the exhilaration of watching the girls' team kicking butt and partially because he hadn't yet calmed down from his own win. The guys' game against Camp Seebar had just ended, and Greg had scored two of his team's five goals. It had taken him a while to get his breathing under control.

Now he was getting worked up all over again.

I've never seen her play like this, Greg realized. Abby executed a perfect assist. Manisha stopped the ball and shot for the goal. It nearly went in, but Camp Seebar's goalie smacked it with her fist at the last moment and sent it flying out-of-bounds.

His eyes were riveted on Abby. Her perfect form, her intense eyes. She was running right toward him . . . and then she passed by, charging the goal. She slammed the ball with the inside of her right foot, and the ball whizzed right past the goalie's left ear and into the net. The whistle blew, and Abby's face lit up as the rest of her team crowded around her, cheering.

As Abby finished shaking hands with the members of the other team, Greg yelled her name and waved his arms, trying to get her attention. She broke away from the crowd, found Greg with her eyes, and grinned.

She ran over to him, jumping into his arms. Greg gave her a tight hug.

Then the strangest thing happened: Greg didn't want to let go. He liked the feel of Abby in his arms . . . a little too much.

Wrong! A warning bell suddenly went off inside his head. He abruptly placed Abby back on the ground.

"Was that not the most incredible thing you've ever seen?" Abby exclaimed, pulling back and grinning so hard that it looked like her face muscles might snap.

Greg's brain was whirling around like a tornado.

What had happened there? "Incredible," he said finally, finding his voice.

"Ahhhhh!" Abby let out a whoop of joy and spun around. "I've never felt like this in my life! I wish Will had been here to see it."

Greg was brought back to reality. *Will, right. Abby likes Will. And I like Joanna. Right.* He looked at Abby and was grateful that the strange connection—whatever it was—seemed to be fading. She was just Abby, and they were just friends. She was practically one of the guys. And he loved her more than anything, but not like that. Loving her like that would just ruin everything. *Chalk it up to that teenage hormonal imbalance insanity they're always warning us about and forget it ever happened.*

"Come on! Let's go get lunch! I am sooooo hungry," Abby said, grabbing his wrist and pulling him along behind a crowd of players on their way down the hill. "I have news."

"What kind of news?" Greg asked. He took a deep breath and let it out slowly. He felt totally normal. Almost.

"Joanna news," Abby told him, practically skipping along the path. "She's totally not mad at you. In fact, she feels bad about stalking off yesterday. She was just mad at Will."

"That's cool," Greg said, smiling as Abby twirled around again. "Will's not mad either, in case you're wondering."

"Thank God!" Abby said. "I didn't really think

he was, 'cause he didn't *seem* mad. But sometimes I just can't read people. Except you, of course." She poked him on the chest playfully. "Why are your ears all red anyway? What'd you do?"

Greg felt his face flush. What was he supposed to tell her? *There was this wacky moment when I wanted to grab you and kiss you . . . but it passed.* He had a feeling that wouldn't go over too well.

"It's just from the game," Greg said. "Sorry to disappoint."

"Darn. I thought you were gonna let me in on some scandal," Abby joked. "But anyway, we're ready for phase three."

"Lay it on me," Greg said.

"You're not gonna like it," Abby said. She stopped and pulled him off the dirt path and onto the grass to let the others pass. "It involves clothes."

"Clothes?"

"Yeah, well, Joanna brought like, seven fashion magazines with her, and she reads them like they're the Bible or something," Abby said.

"So?" Greg prompted.

"So, I got to thinking . . . ," Abby began, averting her eyes and picking a blade of grass. "Maybe you wanna start, I dunno, dressing a little . . . um . . . cooler?"

"I'm gonna pretend I didn't hear that," Greg said, starting to walk again.

"Just hear me out," Abby called, jogging to catch up with him. "Joanna's used to New York guys. And New York guys are sophisticated."

"What are you saying?" Greg asked, starting to get a little angry. He couldn't believe Abby was criticizing the way he dressed. She had practically the same wardrobe he did.

Hey, yeah! "Wait a minute," Greg said. "You're not exactly Cindy Crawford yourself."

"Well, duh. Thanks for the update," Abby said, spreading out her arms to call attention to her maroon-and-black soccer uniform.

"So if I start dressing better, you start dressing better too," Greg challenged, crossing his arms in front of his chest.

"Fine!" Abby said, thrusting out her hand.

Greg clasped her hand and jerked it down. "Fine!"

"Hey, Ab?" Greg said as they continued to weave their way to the mess hall.

"Yeah?"

"Where're we gonna get new clothes?" Greg asked.

"Poor Greg," Abby joked. "You're a little slow on the uptake, aren't you?"

Greg shot her a withering look as they climbed the now familiar mess hall steps.

"Kidding!" Abby said as he opened the door for her. She stopped and faced him. "You get yours from Will, and I'll get mine from Jo. It's cake." Then she started skipping toward their table.

"Ah," Greg said.

But something suddenly occurred to him. He stepped aside to let a group of nine-year-olds loudly singing the Camp Emerson fight song pass by. Abby would be dressing up like Jo to get Will, and he would be dressing up like Will to get Jo. There was something weird going on here.

"Come on, Jo," Abby prodded. "Think of it as a donation to a worthy cause."

"If you came in here with a truck marked Salvation Army, no problem," Joanna said. "But the Abby Wants Will Fund? Sorry. No way. No how." She sat down on top of her trunk and braced her arms on the lid.

"Like you could stop me if I really wanted to get in there," Abby said half jokingly.

Joanna's green eyes flashed. "Just try it," she challenged.

"Ugh!" Abby threw her arms up in exasperation and plopped down on her cot. The springs squealed in protest.

"What're you guys doing?" Jeannie, a petite girl with glossy black hair, was standing in the doorway of their bunk room. They'd gotten back from karaoke night, the night Abby always hid in the corner, about fifteen minutes ago, and Jeannie was already wearing her pink cotton pajamas, her hair pulled into two ponytails. Somehow the look worked.

"I'm trying to get Joanna to let me borrow some clothes," Abby explained, glancing at Joanna hopefully. Maybe her attitude would change with company in the room.

No such luck. Her expression hadn't shifted.

"Oooh! Fashion show!" Jeannie exclaimed, clapping. She bounced into the room and onto the bed next to Abby. The springs squealed again.

"No fashion show," Joanna said. "I'm not lending her anything."

"You're not? But whiiiii . . ." Jeannie's voice trailed off, and her eyes popped open in sheer horror. She was staring right behind Joanna's head.

"What?" Joanna asked, alarmed. "What's wrong?"

Abby glanced over, and her own eyes widened. On the wall, just above Joanna's head, was a hairy spider the size of a silver dollar. And it was crawling toward her.

"Spider!" Jeannie shrieked.

Just as Joanna bolted up and opened her mouth to scream, Abby lunged forward and grabbed a plastic cup off the floor.

"Omigod!" Joanna jumped up and down, trembling violently. "Is it on me? Is it on me? Is it on me?" She leaped onto her bed and shook her arms crazily.

Abby placed the open end of the cup over the spider and slid it down to knock the creature into the bottom of the cup. Then she quickly placed her hand over the top and walked outside into the warm evening air. She hopped down the steps as Joanna's yells began to subside and shook the spider out onto the ground. It just sat there for a minute, probably just as scared as Joanna.

"Thanks, little man," Abby said. "Now I have bargaining power."

Abby pushed through the flimsy screen door and found that Joanna's fit had attracted a crowd. Manisha, Shira, and Allyson had all gathered to see what the commotion was about. Kristen was sitting on Joanna's bed, comforting Jo, who was still twitching.

Abby walked right up to Joanna's trunk and flung it open with a flourish. "Now, what*ever* am I going to wear?" she asked, bringing a finger to her chin and striking a questioning pose. Joanna moaned, but Abby knew it was a sound of resignation. They had made a running deal the first summer they met that if Abby saved Joanna from a fearsome creature—namely, a bug—Joanna would then owe Abby a favor.

The rest of the girls gathered around Abby, and they all gazed into the trunk.

"Wow!" Shira said. "Jo, you've gone way overboard this time."

"Yeah—I just might borrow something of yours for my night off," Kristen joked.

Abby leaned forward, grabbed a black linen shorts set, and held it up to herself. "What do you think, Jo?" she asked. "Is this the kind of outfit that would impress a New York guy?"

Joanna grunted, barely glancing up. "Will is not your average New York guy," she said moodily, staring back at the ground. "He's not your average anything. I can't figure him out at all."

Abby blinked at her friend. She sounded almost depressed. Where did *that* come from?

"It's pretty cool," Allyson said, reaching out to finger the linen. "But I'd lose the sneakers."

"Definitely," Kristen agreed, staring at Abby's feet.

"What do you think, Jo?" Abby asked tentatively.

Joanna took a deep breath and let out a long, slow sigh. Then she hoisted herself off the bed, turned and squatted, and pulled the covers up to reveal a line of shoes. "How about these?" she asked, holding out a pair of chunky-heeled sandals.

"They're perfect," Abby said, kneeling next to her friend. "Are you okay, Jo?" Abby asked, placing a hand on her shoulder. "You look a little green."

"No, I'm all right," Joanna said with a wan smile. "I just . . . I mean it's just . . . Will is . . ." Joanna's voice trailed off, and she looked away.

"Will is what?" Abby asked, totally baffled. For once she couldn't tell if Joanna was being dramatic or if she was really upset. She sure looked like there was something she wanted to say.

"Nothing," Joanna said, standing up. "Why don't you go try that stuff on?"

"Yeah, Ab," Allyson said. "And I think I have the perfect pair of earrings."

Abby stood and cast a quick look at Joanna. She seemed better. Even a little perky.

"Okay," Abby said, taking the sandals from Joanna. "This is so cool. I'm gonna go change in Kristen's room and make a grand entrance." She crossed the room quickly. "I can't wait until

Greg sees me in this. He's gonna just die."

"Greg?" Joanna asked. "You mean Will, right?"

Abby stopped in her tracks and felt a rush of heat rise up her neck. Why had she said Greg?

"Ab?"

"Uh, of course I meant Will. I just, uh, Greg's coming over to see what I picked out." Even as she said it, Abby knew the excuse sounded lame.

"Uh-huh," Kristen said sarcastically. "That's *exactly* it."

Abby walked into Kristen's tiny room, which separated one bunk room from the other. She shut the door behind her and sat down shakily on the cot, feeling almost faint.

Greg. Greg was her best friend. The thought of him wasn't actually making her skin tingle and her knees all mushy, was it?

Forcing herself to conjure up a picture of him in her mind, Abby remembered jumping into his arms after the game. Had something been different?

Abby just sat there as she thought, staring at the wire mesh over the windows and focusing and unfocusing her eyes until she realized that she didn't know. Something *might* have been different.

And that thought scared her—a lot.

"So, is Abby gonna do your makeup for you too?" Will asked, laughing.

"Tell her I recommend purple nail polish," Dominic called from his bed, where he was sealing a letter.

"You should talk, dude," Simon chided. "You're writing to your ball and chain."

Dominic tossed a pillow in Simon's direction, but Greg intercepted it and tossed it back. "Back off, guys," he said, stuffing the clothes Will had loaned him into his gym bag. He couldn't believe he'd actually told them the truth when they'd asked why he'd wanted to borrow clothes. Why couldn't he have come up with a plausible lie?

"Just cover for me with Damon, all right?" Greg asked, pulling the bag onto his shoulder. His eyes darted toward Damon's little room, where the counselor was listening to hip-hop and doing his nightly reps with free weights. "I'll be back by lights-out."

"Yeah. No problem," Will said, looking at Greg with a mocking expression. "We'll tell him you had to run out and get a perm for your big date. Tell her to use the big rollers, Greg. You wouldn't look good all crimped."

The guys laughed, and Simon and Will high-fived.

"You are having way too much fun with this," Greg sneered. He snuck quietly through the door so Damon wouldn't hear him.

Greg hurried along the path that led around the lake to the girls' cabins, cursing Abby's little fashion show idea for the millionth time. Will was never going to let him live this down. He was probably back at the cabin right now, brainstorming new and demeaning jokes with the others.

81

"It's no big deal," Greg muttered to himself. "If this doesn't work, I'll just kill her." He laughed. "Or sue her for defamation of character."

He ducked under the low branches of an oak tree and took a deep breath as Abby's cabin came into view. At least Will had let him take whatever he wanted. Greg hadn't been sure if a sweater vest would be overdoing it, so his bag was stuffed with a bunch of different choices. He just hoped Abby would approve something quick so he could put this whole thing behind him and get back to the cabin before Damon realized he was gone or Babs caught him outside his cabin.

As Greg ascended the steps and crossed the small porch to the door of Abby's cabin, laughter floated through the screen windows. All different kinds of laughter. Girls' laughter.

Startled, Greg moved aside and flattened himself against the wall next to the door. Joanna was probably in there. Why hadn't he thought of that? *Obviously* she was in there—she lived in Abby's bunk. Greg looked down at his overstuffed bag. How was he supposed to explain why he had a sack full of Will's clothes without coming off as a total geek?

"This is so stupid. I'm outta here," Greg muttered. He had just pushed himself away from the wall and taken a step when he heard the door swing open behind him. Busted.

Greg turned around slowly, searching his brain for an explanation for his presence. But when he saw Abby standing in the doorway, all excuses flew out of his mind.

"Hi," Abby said tentatively.

A weird tingly sensation shot up Greg's spine, and he was absently aware that his mouth was hanging open and no sound was coming out. He felt his ears flare up, and he glanced around quickly, guiltily, as if the girls gathered in the doorway could read his thoughts.

She's completely gorgeous, he thought.

Abby was wearing a little black tank top that showed just a touch of her tanned midriff and a pair of impossibly short matching shorts. Her hair was brushed out and fanned around her shoulders, and she had on a pair of dangly silver earrings that made her eyes sparkle. Plus she was taller. Greg glanced down at her feet and saw that she was wearing a pair of strappy, high-heeled sandals that made her toned legs look even more shapely. He started sweating.

"So? What do you think?" Abby asked.

What do I think? Greg's mind screamed. *I think I've finally lost it!*

"Greg?" Joanna prompted him. She was now standing next to Abby. The rest of the girls stared at him.

"Yeah?" Greg said, having no idea what he was supposed to say. He was tongue-tied and totally confused. It wasn't like he hadn't seen Abby dressed up before. It was just, well, in that outfit she was definitely *not* one of the guys. She was more like a homecoming queen. Greg's heart thudded against his chest, and he wiped his palms on his cotton T-shirt.

"Well, how do you like Abby's new look?" Joanna asked with a smile.

Greg locked eyes with Abby for a moment. She looked excited but a little bit unsure. He had to tell her the truth.

"You look beautiful," he said, still staring right into her eyes.

All the girls burst into giggles. Greg's entire body turned red.

Abby blushed and smiled, her eyes never leaving his face. "Thanks," she said simply, looking relieved and ecstatic.

"You look beautiful," someone in the cabin mocked in a fake deep voice.

Greg felt sick to his stomach over his total lack of coolness. They were laughing at him. "I gotta, uh, I gotta go," he mumbled, backing up. "Damon doesn't know I'm gone, and I . . . uh . . . I gotta get back."

Abby looked as if she was about to say something, but before she could make a sound, Greg turned on his heels and fled.

Eight

"THIS IS A joke, right?" Greg asked Abby. "There's, like, a hidden camera in here or something."

"Come on, Greg, it's not that bad. Just pretend it's an Easter egg," Abby suggested, taking a seat on a stool.

She watched Greg look down at the plain ceramic bowl in front of him. It was Saturday morning, and it was pouring outside, so everyone had been forced to choose an indoor activity. Abby had convinced Greg to come to the arts and crafts cabin with her.

She was in a great mood. Not only had she done bowl decorating every summer and enjoyed it, but she was also sitting next to Greg and not experiencing a single mushy feeling. She'd been worried about hanging out with him ever since her slip of the tongue the night before. But now she was glad that things seemed to be back to normal. Greg was just Greg.

"When I saw your bowls at your house, I

didn't think they made *guys* do this," Greg whined, lowering himself onto his stool and trailing his eyes over the cups of paint in front of them. He picked up a brush and looked at it as if it were an alien being.

A couple of younger campers ran by, chasing each other with paint-covered sponges. Teddy Barber, who was helping the art counselor keep an eye on things, grabbed them around the waist and planted each one on a stool. Abby blushed when Teddy gave her a small smile.

She returned her attention to Greg. "What kinds of crafts did you think guys would do here?" she asked, dipping her brush in a vat of yellow paint. "Painting nudes?"

On cue Greg's ears turned red. "No. But there's always wood shop. You know, big, loud, sharp tools. Hammers and things. Guy stuff."

Abby rolled her eyes. "What century are you from anyway?"

"I don't know. But I'm not doing anything like that." He gestured at an example bowl in the center of the wooden table. It had been painted a light violet color and was decorated with little daisies.

"Um, I don't think you're expected to paint flowers, Greg," Abby said, putting down the brush and rolling up the sleeves of her mothball-scented smock. "Look at Simon over there." She nodded in Simon's direction. He was sitting one table over, concentrating on covering a bowl with dark blue paint. "Do something manly if you want."

"Manly?" Greg asked, smirking.

"Yeah. A bowl can be manly." Abby smiled. Greg could be so cute when he was intimidated. It was just funny that paintbrushes intimidated him while six-foot-four soccer guards with five o'clock shadows and a lust for blood didn't at all.

"Huh. All right. A manly bowl it is," Greg said. He dipped a large brush into the black paint and came out with a huge glob, which he dropped into the bottom of his bowl. Then he started to spread it around, evening it out along the inside walls.

"What're you gonna do?" Abby asked, peeking in his bowl as he worked.

"None of your business," Greg answered. "You, as a girl, wouldn't understand."

Abby smiled and returned to coating her own bowl with the light yellow, quick-drying paint. "Speaking of not understanding," she said, stealing a glance at him out of the corner of her eye, "why did you bolt so quickly last night? I never got a chance to see the stuff Will lent you."

Abby concentrated on her work but was aware that Greg was shifting uncomfortably in his seat. There was a loud crash from across the room, and Abby almost jumped out of her smock. She laughed and immediately found Simon with her eyes. He was standing over a few dozen shattered pieces of bowl.

"Nice one, Simon," Greg called.

"Thanks, Neill," Simon answered with a smile. He bent to clean up the mess.

"He does that at least once a year," Abby said. "So anyway, why did you run off last night?"

87

"I, well, Joanna was there," Greg said, dipping his brush in the black paint again. "And I figured it would probably be a bad idea for her to see me showing you all that stuff, ya know? I thought it would have a negative effect on my coolness quotient."

"Oh, I didn't think of that," Abby said. She wiped her brush on a paper towel and studied the paints, trying to figure out what to do next. Flowers? Hearts? Soccer balls? "But Kristen wouldn't have let you inside anyway. I could've just looked at the clothes on the porch."

"I guess," Greg said. He stopped working and blew his bangs out of his face. "It just freaked me out a little, having all those girls there staring and getting all giggly."

Abby felt a little twinge of disappointment in the pit of her stomach that she couldn't quite explain. It made sense that Greg had been uncomfortable. But after the way his jaw had dropped when he'd seen her all dressed up, she'd kind of thought *she* had gotten him all flustered. It would've been cool to know she could inspire that kind of reaction in a member of the male sex.

"Anyway," Greg said, working on the outside of the bowl, "Joanna probably thinks I'm a moron after watching me run away like that."

Abby was pulled out of her thoughts. "Don't worry about that," she said. "I'm sure Joanna likes you."

Greg put down his brush and leaned back a little, examining his work. "Why do you think she likes me? Has she said anything?"

Abby paused to think, painting a little heart on the newspaper that covered the table. Aside from mentioning that she felt bad for ditching him in the woods, Joanna hadn't really mentioned Greg at all.

"Uh, well, not exactly," she said, reaching for the white paint and avoiding his eyes. "But she hasn't said she *doesn't* like you." She looked over at Greg, expecting him to look dejected. But he was just sitting there, painting away, appearing totally unfazed.

Wow. He doesn't seem worried in the least, Abby thought. She envied his confidence.

"So, does Will ever mention me?" she asked, trying to sound nonchalant.

Greg hesitated and shifted in his seat. The rubber soles of his sneakers squeaked against the stool's footrest. "Well, when he heard the way you dominated at the game the other day, he said he wished he'd been there," Greg said finally.

Abby's face fell. She twisted her paintbrush around in the white paint and then started to apply little dots to the side of her bowl. "Oh, well," she said, sighing. "We still have the whole month."

"Totally. Don't worry, Ab," Greg said, touching his bowl lightly with his fingertips to test if the paint had dried. "I'm sure he'll fall at your feet when he sees you in that outfit at the theater later. We're talking drool inducing."

Abby grinned. "So you did like the outfit," she said, rolling her brush between her hands. "I thought I was so hideous, I scared you away."

89

"I *told* you, I left because I felt like an idiot. Not because you *looked* like an idiot."

Abby glanced over at Greg and almost cracked up laughing. He was squinting into the bottom of his bowl, and his tongue was sticking out of the side of his mouth. As if *that* was helping him concentrate.

"Talk about looking like an idiot," Abby quipped. Greg shot her a scathing look as he dipped a tiny brush in a cup of silver paint. "Do you need any help?" she asked.

"Don't interrupt an artist at work," Greg deadpanned. He wiped the excess paint off the brush on the rim of the cup, then leaned over the bowl and started painting carefully in the base. Abby was dying to look over his shoulder. He was so intent— she could tell it was taking serious effort for him to hold his hand steady.

Finally he put down his brush and held up the bowl for her inspection. Abby gasped. "Greg! That is so cool!" she said in awe. He'd painted a perfect replica of Superman's *S* sign in the bottom of his bowl.

"Well, you said do something manly. And it doesn't get more manly than that," he told her in a superlow voice.

Abby laughed. Greg was so awesome. She hoped Joanna appreciated how lucky she was to have caught his attention. Greg had only dated two girls in the past, and they'd both bored him pretty quickly. But every girl in their class wanted him . . . and they were all jealous of Abby because they thought she and Greg were made for each other. True, she could see how they'd seem that way to an outsider, but she and Greg would be disastrous as a couple. He was just . . . well . . . *she* was just . . . they were completely—

"What're you thinkin'?" Greg asked suddenly, wiping his hands on a clean rag.

Abby blushed and turned back to her work, thinking it might be funny to tell him the truth. *I was unsuccessfully trying to come up with a reason why we shouldn't be together.* Once again she remembered calling Will Greg the night before, and her face burned even hotter.

"Nothing," she answered. "Just that you were born to paint."

"Thanks," Greg said, smiling. "So, Ab, can I ask you a question?" He turned in his seat so that he was completely facing her.

"Uh, of course," Abby mumbled. For some reason her hands were shaking, so she decided to give up on painting for the moment. Instead she folded her fingers in her lap and looked up at him.

"Why do you like Will anyway?" he asked. He picked his bowl up and held it in front of his face, blowing on the design in the bottom. "I mean, he doesn't seem like your type."

Abby had to laugh at that. "My type? How would you know what my type is? I've never even *had* a boyfriend. *I* don't even know what my type is."

"I know. I know," Greg said, nodding and replacing his bowl on the table. "I mean, I just always imagined you with a guy who would, you know, like, take you to ball games, shoot hoops in the driveway. Not a guy who falls all over himself on a fifteen-minute hike."

Abby's stomach turned. "Jeez, Greg. You make it sound like I'm not even a girl."

"That's not what I meant," Greg said adamantly. His green eyes looked slightly pained. "I didn't mean that at all. I just, I don't know. I don't think Will would like doing all that stuff. You know, all the stuff—"

"You mean all the stuff *we* do together, right?" Abby asked, looking down.

Greg laughed. "I didn't really think of it that way, but yeah."

Abby was having a hard time locating her tongue. Was the stuff she and Greg did together couple-type stuff? And if it was—

"Ab?"

Abby shook herself out of her thoughts. "C'mon, Greg," she said, picking up her paintbrush again. "That's kid stuff. I mean, even you have to admit there's more to life than wrestling and noogies and—"

"What's *that* supposed to mean?" Greg demanded. He tensed up so quickly, Abby could feel the shift in the air. His eyes flashed.

"I mean, rolling around in the dirt isn't exactly romantic," Abby said with a shrug. "I just—"

"Oh, that's rich, Abby," Greg said fiercely, pushing back his stool. "Now that you're all in love with a New York guy, you think you're too sophisticated to hang out with me, right?"

Abby blanched. She'd never seen Greg get so

worked up. And who said she was *in love* with Will? "Greg, I . . . I didn't mean—"

"Forget it," Greg said quickly. He placed his hands on his hips and stared at her as if contemplating whether or not to say anything else. He looked almost disappointed in her.

Abby chewed on her bottom lip to keep herself from blurting an explanation. He obviously didn't want to hear it.

"Just . . . just forget I said anything," he said finally, sounding resigned. He grabbed his bowl and placed it on one of the drying shelves, then yanked off his smock and tossed it in the large box with the others. Abby watched in confusion as he walked across the room and started chatting with Simon, who was still working on his project.

"Wow. Who are you, and what have you done with my best friend?" Abby joked to herself.

She felt bad for having offended him, but what was the big deal? If she started dating someone, it wasn't like she was going to stop hanging out with Greg and doing the usual stuff. You'd think he was afraid of losing her to another guy or something. And that wasn't possible—because she and Greg *were not* a couple.

Nine

"SO YOU FORGIVE me?" Abby asked as she and Greg walked through the side door into the theater.

Greg laughed. "As long as you forgive me for my little . . . uh . . . outburst," he said, feeling like a total moron. He pushed aside a rust-colored curtain that led to the stage and held it for Abby to walk through.

"It never happened," she said, smiling. "Maybe you were just PMS-ing."

"Hey—"

"Kidding!" Abby exclaimed, throwing up her hands.

Greg let his shoulders relax for the first time since the art-room incident. After a strained lunch, during which Joanna and Will hadn't even looked at each other and Greg had purposely sat between Jeannie and Manisha to avoid talking to Abby, he'd really needed to set things straight. He couldn't believe he'd actually thrown a tantrum in public. Abby had been pointing out that everything they did together was immature, and Greg had practically proved her right by acting like a complete child. Him—Greg Neill—the guy who'd merely asked for a safety pin when his shorts had ripped in gym, exposing his red Hanes briefs. The guy who was known for never, ever, under any circumstances showing emotion in public. But as long as Abby had forgiven him, all was right with the world.

"Hey! There's Will!" Abby said excitedly. Greg saw that Will was roaming in circles near the back of the stage, mumbling as he read from a tattered script.

"How do I look?" Abby asked, hopping a few feet in front of Greg so that he could check her out.

"Great," Greg told her, stuffing his hands into the pockets of Will's khaki shorts to avoid reaching out and stretching her shirt down to cover her midriff. Did Will really need to see so much of her perfect figure? And why had Joanna brought clothes like that to camp anyway?

"Wish me luck!" she stage-whispered, then took off in Will's direction.

Greg exhaled. He watched as Will smiled at Abby and let his eyes roam shamelessly over her new outfit. Will laughed loudly at something she said, and Abby giggled like a schoolgirl. When Will reached over to tuck a strand of hair behind Abby's ear, Greg decided it was time to check out backstage.

His hands were shaking, so he crossed his arms over Will's forest green polo shirt as he shuffled through the left wing to the backstage area. It was a huge space, big enough to be a second stage, and there were already tons of sets in various degrees of construction. Some of the other volunteers were spreading out tarps and opening large cans of paint.

Greg looked down at his clothes. The crisp shorts, the spotless shirt, the practically mooing leather docksiders. "I can't paint in these clothes," he said aloud.

Shira walked by him, carrying a freshly painted tree. She was holding it at full arm's length away from her body.

"If you're gonna hang around, you'd better go change," she told him. "We're known for our spontaneous paint fights."

Greg groaned. "Thanks for the tip."

Swiftly he headed back toward the wings, figuring he might be able to avoid work altogether if he found the right hiding place. He spotted a large crate in a dark corner and sat down on top of it, leaning back against the cool brick wall.

His thoughts returned to his outburst the day before. He'd spent half the night awake, staring at the ceiling of his cabin and wondering why Abby's comment had upset him so much. Who cared if she thought the stuff they did together was unsophisticated? It wasn't like he needed to impress her. They'd been friends forever. She'd seen him in his Spider-Man jammies when he was little. She'd been there when Seth and David—the evil Rosen twins—had beaten him up and stolen his Big Wheel. She knew that he hadn't figured out how to tie his own shoes until he was nine years old. There was no way he could impress her even if he wanted to. She knew too much.

"And why would I want to impress her?" he asked himself for the zillionth time. "It's not like we're dating."

But every time Greg got to this point in his train of thought, he remembered his little twilight zone experience on the soccer field the other day . . . and the way he'd started sweating profusely when he'd first seen Abby in her little black outfit. And the fact that he'd been holding his breath when she leaned in close to him in the art room. There was only one explanation for all of that: recurring temporary insanity.

"I can't like Abby. We're buds. I like Joanna."

Where was Joanna anyway? Greg pushed himself up and sauntered over toward the stage. He was just peeking around the curtain when he heard someone approach him from behind. Before he could turn, a hand covered his eyes.

"Guess who?" Joanna asked with a feebly disguised voice.

Greg decided to play along. He sniffed the air. "Well, you *smell* pretty good," he said. Her perfume smelled like spring flowers without being overwhelming.

"Oh, Greg." She slapped him lightly on the shoulder. "You're so silly."

He turned to look at her and smiled. She was wearing a red T-shirt and a short skirt. Her strawberry blond hair was pushed back in a headband, showing off her perfect skin.

"I love your shirt, Greg," she gushed, pulling him out onto the stage, where it was lighter. "That color totally matches your eyes," she said loudly.

Greg blushed as Joanna reached up to straighten his collar. He glanced over at Abby at the back of the stage, where she was still hanging with Will. She and Will were both looking right at them.

Good. She noticed, Greg thought, his heart rate accelerating slightly. *But wait . . . why do I care?*

"Check it out!" Greg said, pulling a fedora hat over one eye. "Indiana Jones."

"Cute," Abby said moodily. "But you can't exactly use it to cover your clothes."

"Sorry," Greg said, returning the hat to a shelf. "How're we supposed to know what's good and what's junk anyway?"

"This, I would say, is junk," Abby said, pulling a lime green housecoat from the rack.

"You don't know that," Greg said. "What if there's a play that has a grandmother?"

Abby shrugged and shoved the ugly robe back on the rack with the rest of the stuff. She was getting irritated and wished she could snag some time alone. She needed some time to think and to try to figure out why Joanna's little performance with Greg's collar had upset her so much. When she'd heard Jo's comment about Greg's eyes and seen her touching him that way, she'd felt a twinge of something that felt a whole lot like jealousy. That was a concept that Abby could *not* deal with. Especially not with Greg hanging over her shoulder.

Greg knelt down and pulled a box out from under the hanging clothes. Abby watched him out of the corner of her eye and was suddenly struck with an idea. Maybe it *was* jealousy. But maybe she was just jealous that her two best friends were getting closer. Maybe, deep in the recesses of her mind, she was afraid that Greg and Jo would get together and leave her behind. She'd read enough *Seventeen* magazines in her day to know that this basically happened all the time.

Abby let out a deep breath. *Yeah, that must be it,* she told herself. Greg bent over to rummage through a box, and Abby suddenly noticed how . . . *flattering* Will's shorts were on him. *Okay. So why do I keep checking out his bod?*

"Maybe we should just go over to the art cabin and grab some smocks," Greg said, standing back up.

Wow, Abby thought as he looked at her, *his eyes really do match that shirt.*

"Will! Quit it! Get off me!" Joanna's voice suddenly floated through the auditorium. Abby glanced in the direction of the stage and then back at Greg.

He raised an eyebrow. "I'm intrigued," he said.

They jogged from the costume room, through the backstage area, and into the wings. Will and

Joanna were out on the stage running scenes, and the backstage crew had been expressly warned not to disturb rehearsal.

Abby snuck forward, with Greg right behind her, and peeked around the curtains. Joanna and Will were standing at center stage, the spotlight fixed on them. Will was staring at the rafters in an obvious attempt at controlling his temper, and Joanna was squinting out at the seats with her hands on her hips.

"Ms. Marshall, I . . . I'm not ready to practice the kiss yet," Joanna stammered.

"What?" Greg whispered. Abby started to get out of his way so he could get a better look, but as he stepped forward his foot caught on a papier-mâché rock and he reached out to Abby, a panicked look in his eyes.

Abby tried to catch him, but his sudden weight spun her around and sent them both tumbling over, their arms wrapped around each other.

Abby was aware of a loud crash just before she was lying on her side, tangled up with Greg, covered in something cold, wet, and sticky.

"Ugh!" she groaned, opening her eyes. Her mouth dropped open in horror. "Oh, no," she said.

Greg was covered in brown paint. It was in his hair, all over Will's shirt—even his little leg hairs were matted to his skin with the stuff. Which could only mean . . . Abby looked down. Yep. They were sitting on a flattened cardboard tree.

"Oh. My. God." Joanna was standing over

them, an expression of absolute shock on her face, with Will and Ms. Marshall at her sides.

Abby slowly turned her head to look at Greg. They both burst out laughing.

Greg sat up and pointed at Abby, overcome with heaving laughter.

"You should see yourself!" Abby exclaimed, her eyes tearing up.

"I can't believe you think this is funny!" Joanna shouted. "Look! Look what you've done to my clothes!"

Abby immediately caught her breath. She knew there was almost nothing in this world more important to Joanna than her wardrobe. "Joanna, I'm so—"

"Forget your stupid outfit!" Will bellowed, throwing his hands in the air. "They've totally broken my concentration. I'm done now. Totally done. Useless for the rest of the day." He rolled up his script and tossed it across the stage.

"Oh, you're useless anyway!" Joanna fumed. "All you care about is getting your handsome face in the spotlight."

Will stared back at her for a moment, his mouth forming into a smirk. "So, you think I'm handsome?" he asked.

Joanna turned beet red. "That's not . . . it's not what I meant," she said, putting her hands on her hips.

"Yeah? Well, I may be a spotlight hog, but you're totally unprofessional!" Will retorted. "You won't even practice the kiss? What's up with that?"

"I just don't think . . . I mean, you . . ." Joanna stopped and cleared her throat. "If I kissed you, you wouldn't be able to handle it," she said defiantly.

Will opened his mouth to retort, but all that came out was a little squeak.

Abby winced. Will looked pretty embarrassed. Joanna gave him a triumphant glare and stalked off the stage.

"I'm outta here," Will said finally. He walked across the stage shakily, picking up his script on the way.

"Actors," Ms. Marshall quipped in a calm voice. Then she glanced down at Abby and Greg. "Why don't you two get cleaned up? On Monday we'll discuss your new roles in the theater program."

"New roles?" they repeated in unison.

"There has to be something you guys can do that's risk-free," Ms. Marshall said. Then she walked away, shaking her head as she went.

Abby smiled slightly at Greg. "Oops."

"Yeah," he said. "Oops is an understatement."

Ten

"OKAY, *HOW DO* you do this?" Greg asked after his third marshmallow melted off his stick and hit the ground with a plop. This was, without a doubt, the most frustrating culinary experience of his life.

"*Now* will you let me help you?" Abby asked jovially.

Greg looked around the campfire at the rest of the senior campers, who were happily munching away on white goo. His stomach rumbled angrily. It was Sunday night. Dinner had been fine, but he had a feeling he'd be hungry for the rest of his life after the workout he'd endured. Officially Sunday was reserved for sports, but they might as well put "boot camp" on the schedule instead.

"Fine, Your Camp Highness," he said finally, handing her the long, thin branch. It was charred at the end, with little bits of hardened marshmallow stuck all over it. "Please enlighten me," he joked.

Abby scooted forward slightly so she was sitting right next to Greg, reaching over him to grab the big bag of marshmallows. Her knee grazed his, and he felt a tingling sensation shoot down his leg and then overtake his whole body.

Just ignore it, Greg told himself. *It's not really there.*

"Okay, first of all, you have to make sure you get the center of the marshmallow," Abby explained, demonstrating slowly.

Greg found himself focusing on her lips. *What would she do if I just grabbed her and kissed her?* he wondered. *She'd probably be so shocked, she'd just kiss me back. She'd probably be happy. She'd probably—*

"Greg? Are you even listening to me?" Abby asked suddenly.

She'd probably kill me, Greg thought, rubbing his forehead with his hand in agitation.

"Sorry. I just zoned," Greg said, shooting her an apologetic look.

Abby rolled her eyes good-naturedly. She handed him a marshmallow on a stick and quickly assembled another one.

"Now just hold it exactly where I hold mine," she directed, stretching her marshmallow toward the fire. Greg thrust his arm out.

"Don't charbroil it!" Abby scolded. She grabbed his arm and pulled it back.

Greg jerked away. "I can do it," he said testily. *Just stop touching me!* he screamed silently.

"Touchy, touchy," Abby said, refocusing her attention on her own marshmallow.

Greg took a deep breath, inhaling the heady scent of the roaring fire. On his way over here tonight he'd been determined to get his mind off Abby. But he knew the warning signs. The sweaty palms, the pounding heart, the sick feeling he got in his stomach when he saw her with Will. There was no denying it anymore—he had a crush on his best friend.

Rolling his shoulders to loosen some tense muscles, Greg looked around to make sure Joanna hadn't decided to make a late arrival. Kristen was starting to tell a ghost story that was attracting a small crowd around her, but Jo wasn't among them.

That girl was foiling his whole plan. He'd thought that if he could spend some quality flirt time with Joanna in front of the fire and totally focus his attention on her, he'd forget his scary developing feelings for Abby. But no. Jo's parents had to show up unexpectedly tonight and take her out to dinner.

"At least Will's not here either," Greg mumbled.

"What?"

Greg's ears fired up. He hadn't realized he'd spoken out loud.

"Uh, I was just wishing Jo and Will were here," Greg said quickly. At least it was half true.

"I'm not good enough company?" Abby asked, raising her eyebrows.

Greg had a sudden vision of his foot being stuffed into his mouth. "No, it's not that," he said, grasping for something to say. "I just figured the atmosphere might get them in the mood to forgive us."

Abby's face relaxed. She looked over at the flames. Greg couldn't help noticing how her skin glowed in the firelight. . . .

"They're done," she said. Greg refocused his attention and found that he had just roasted a perfect marshmallow.

"Hey! Check it out," he said proudly, pulling it toward him.

"Blow on it first," Abby cautioned. Greg complied. He was just psyched he was finally going to get to eat.

"I can't believe Will would rather rehearse by himself than hang out at a campfire with me," Abby said. She tested the marshmallow with her tongue.

That is too cute, Greg thought. Then he gave himself a mental slap. *Get over it!*

"Yeah, uh, me neither," he said. "But he and Jo were pretty mad."

Abby pulled her snack off the stick, brought it to her mouth, and started munching, taking little tiny bites. She looked just like a baby rabbit.

"So, what do we do now?" Abby asked. "I tried to apologize to Joanna, but she still sat at the other end of the table during dinner."

"Well, I have a little plan for Jo," Greg said, biting off half his marshmallow. Maybe he could get this night focused on Joanna after all. Then he'd stop thinking about how cute Abby looked with that little drip of melted goo on her chin. . . .

Against his better judgment, Greg reached over and wiped Abby's chin gently with his thumb—a movement that would have seemed normal to him a couple of days ago. But now it was charged with excitement.

Before he even had time to take his hand away, his eyes locked with Abby's. He froze. Had she felt it too?

Abby blinked. "So, what's your Joanna plan?"

Guess not.

Greg wiped his hands on his denim shorts and cleared his throat. "I'm gonna tell her it was all my fault—that I grabbed you before we fell and that I'm sorry," he explained in what he hoped was a confident voice.

Abby laughed loudly and licked her fingertips. "*That's* your plan?"

Instantly Greg felt defensive. He'd really thought this out. "Don't underestimate me, Ab—I have three older sisters. You can't live in my house and not absorb some vital information about women."

"Then maybe I should talk to them," Abby said, a smile in her eyes, "'cause somehow I don't see confession of guilt as a turn-on."

"Show's how much you know," Greg joked. "My sisters totally gush when a guy admits he's wrong. They fall all over themselves—especially if he brings flowers. It's embarrassing, actually."

The corners of Abby's mouth twitched down as

if she were contemplating his words. "I have to admit, that is inspired," she said, pulling her knees up under her chin and wrapping her arms around her legs. "But what about Will?"

Just forget about him, Greg thought. *He's not good enough for you anyway.*

"I mean, I doubt my taking the blame will cut it," Abby said.

And who is good enough for her—you? a little voice mocked. *That's a laugh. You're such a wuss, you can't even tell her how you feel.*

"I don't feel anything," Greg protested through clenched teeth.

"About what?"

"Huh?"

"You don't feel anything about what?" Abby prodded, her brows knit together. Her blue eyes looked wary as the firelight reflected in them.

Great. Now she thinks I'm schizo.

Then it hit him, out of nowhere—like a soccer ball to the head. He knew exactly what to do.

"I have an idea," he said, snapping his fingers.

"You do?" Abby looked skeptical.

"Yeah. Yeah, I do." Greg was getting excited. It was a stroke of genius. He couldn't have planned it out better if he'd thought about it all night. It was a plan that would prove to Abby once and for all that she and Will were the most ill-conceived couple in the history of the world.

"You should offer to rehearse with him," he said, sitting up straight.

Abby arched one eyebrow. "What're you on, Neill?" she asked. "You want him to run screaming from the room?"

"No! Listen!" Greg said excitedly, grabbing the arms of her blue windbreaker. Almost everyone was gathered around Kristen for story time now, but he lowered his voice anyway, to make sure no one heard his plan. "It's perfect." *So perfect!* "Will's mad because we interrupted rehearsal. And all he cares about is practicing. That's the whole reason he's not here right now."

Abby nodded slowly, as if she were processing the idea. "And practicing with someone else is probably better than running lines alone."

"Exactly!" Greg said, releasing her arms. She was gonna do it. He could tell by the intrigued look on her face. And once Will saw how completely inept Abby was when faced with a script, he'd realize they had nothing in common and forget all about her. Sure, Abby might be hurt at first, but she'd get over it. It would be better for her in the long run, right? Better to find out sooner than later and all that. It was flawless!

"Maybe we could rehearse the kissing scene!" Abby squealed, clapping excitedly.

Or . . . less than flawless.

"Are you ever going to speak to me again?" Abby asked Joanna on Monday morning, glancing at her friend's reflection in the dingy mirror above the sinks.

"Maybe," Joanna said through a mouthful of toothpaste.

Abby slathered moisturizing cream over her face. "Maybe you *will* talk to me again, or maybe you *won't* talk to me again?"

Joanna rolled her eyes and spit into the white ceramic sink. "Don't you already do enough talking for both of us?" she asked.

"Ha! You talked to me!" Abby cheered, thrusting a finger at her. "That means you're forgiving me!"

"Your train of thought is numbing my brain," Joanna said with a small smirk.

Abby laughed. "I really am sorry, Joanna," she told her, rubbing some excess moisturizer off on her arm. "I'll pay you back someday."

"Whatever." Joanna wiped her mouth on a plush pink facecloth. "It's just clothes." She fluffed up her bangs with her fingers, then squinted at her reflection.

Abby covered her heart with her hand, reeling back in only partially feigned shock.

"Oh, shut up." Joanna grinned before Abby could even come up with a good line.

Abby couldn't help smiling as she pulled her hair back in a ponytail. Things were returning to normal with Joanna, and Greg's plan for her and Will was inspired. Plus she had almost forgotten about that weird attraction to Greg she'd felt at the theater.

Of course, there *had* been that moment of mind-blowing electricity at the campfire last night, when he'd wiped a glob of marshmallow off her chin.

But Greg likes Joanna, and I like Will. It must've been my imagination, or the campfire light, or maybe the marshmallows were old and they infected my brain.

Abby cast a sidelong glance at Joanna, who was now flossing with a vengeance.

"So, um, Greg's really sorry too," Abby said, mostly to see Joanna's reaction.

"Really?" Joanna said. She stopped flossing and licked her teeth, studying them in the mirror.

"Yeah," Abby continued, feeling slightly guilty. Greg probably wanted to tell Joanna how he felt himself, but it was just like when Abby was faced with a full box of Famous Amos chocolate chip cookies—she couldn't stop herself until she was done. "He feels like it's all his fault, and he wants to take you on a date to apologize."

Joanna's face lit up. Abby's heart constricted. *I guess Greg's plan was right on,* she thought.

"A date?" Joanna squeaked. She always squeaked when she was really excited.

"Well, as real as a date can be at camp," Abby said. Jeez. She sounded like such a wet rag.

"This is perfect," Joanna said thoughtfully. She looked as though she were contemplating an issue larger than a date. "This just might work."

"Whaddaya mean?" Abby asked. Why did everybody seem to be talking in code lately?

"Oh, nothing," Joanna said with a wave of her

hand. Abby noticed that Jo was blushing slightly and that her green eyes were shining with excitement. "I have to go figure out what to wear! Thanks, Ab!" Joanna grabbed Abby in a quick hug, then bolted from the bathroom.

Slowly, dejectedly, Abby looked at herself in the mirror. What was wrong with her? Why couldn't she just forget the momentary attraction she'd felt for Greg and be happy for her friends?

Because it wasn't just temporary, a little voice inside her head whispered. *You're just jealous. Admit it, and get on with your life.*

"You can't be jealous of Joanna," she told her reflection. "That would mean you had an actual crush on Greg, and, I'm sorry, but that's just not possible. That would just put an end to life as we know it, and I, for one, can't deal with that kind of pressure."

With that, Abby gave herself a terse nod and marched out of the bathroom.

Greg let the handle of his blue toothbrush hang out of his mouth as he watched Will shave under his chin. He was totally riveted. How did people do that without slitting their own throats?

"What's your problem, Neill?" Will asked, stopping in midshave. "You've never seen a guy with facial hair before?"

Greg quickly averted his eyes and continued brushing his teeth vigorously. Then he rinsed out his mouth and wiped the sides of his lips with his hand. "No. I just . . . how long have you been shaving anyway?" he asked, holding his toothbrush under the faucet.

"Since about seventh grade," Will answered, shaking the razor under a stream of water. "Trust me, man, it's not fun. You should be happy you're not naturally hairy like me."

"Yeah, right," Greg said, shooting Will an irritated look. The guy sounded just like Greg's father when he told him he couldn't practice driving on the family's new BMW. "It's too big a responsibility," his father would say. "Once you had it, you wouldn't want it." Sure. Like Greg would really regret being able to cruise down Lakeside Drive with the top down and the radio blasting. Wasn't that what every guy wanted out of life? Greg laughed under his breath and shook his head. It would be a revelation for the record books if one day when he became "an adult," he understood everything that everyone now told him he'd understand when he was older.

"What's so funny?" Will asked defensively, glaring at Greg.

Greg noticed there was a dot of blood on Will's chin. *Well, at least he's not good at it.*

"Nothing," Greg answered. He leaned back on the grimy sink and crossed his arms over his chest. "I just remembered something funny my dad said once."

"Good, because I was beginning to think that my sole purpose for being here this summer was to amuse you," Will shot back.

Greg winced. "Listen, man—we didn't interrupt your rehearsal on purpose. I swear," he said. "Abby and I are just seriously uncoordinated."

"Right. Uncoordinated stellar athletes. Good luck with your soccer career." Will glanced in the mirror, saw the blood, and then crossed to the blue-walled toilet stalls. He returned with a scrap of toilet paper and stuck it over the spot.

"I know how it sounds, but it's true," Greg said, laughing. "I'm trying to apologize here, man. Give me a break."

Will took a deep breath. "It's cool, man," he said. "It was just bad timing, ya know?"

Greg gave Will a questioning look, wondering what he meant.

"I've just been looking forward to doing that scene," Will said, rinsing his hands. "If I had just gotten Joanna to kiss me—"

Greg's eyebrows shot up.

"I mean . . . if you can get through a tense scene like that . . . uh . . . it sometimes makes it easier to work with the other person," Will explained.

Greg nodded. He didn't get acting at all, but he supposed that made sense. "And working with Joanna isn't exactly easy," Greg supplied. He grabbed his brush and ran it through his unruly hair.

"You don't do her justice." Will smirked. "She's impossible." He plucked the little white scrap of paper off his chin and inspected the spot in the mirror.

"Well . . . would more rehearsal time help?" Greg asked, eyeing Will discreetly for his reaction. Greg knew that Will rehearsed basically all the time. The other day he'd even gotten out of swimming, his minor, by faking an asthma attack.

"Sure, but I've *been* rehearsing whenever they'll let me. You know that. I've gotten out of every evening activity so that I can rehearse after dinner." Will gathered up his things and started stuffing them into his leather overnight bag. "It just doesn't help much when there's no one to cue you."

"Cue you?" Greg asked.

"Feed you lines," Will explained. "You know, like, it would be hard practicing passing and assists if there was no one there to practice with."

"Right! Duh," Greg scolded himself. "But, well, Abby sort of had an idea about that. I don't know if you'll go for it, but . . ." Greg trailed off, suddenly doubting the merits of his plan. He could really be setting both Abby and Will up for an uncomfortable scenario.

"What is it?" Will asked as Greg threw his toothbrush, paste, soap, and a few other things into a plastic A & P bag.

"She figured maybe she could get permission to run lines with you one night. I mean, she's not the best actress, but—"

"That's perfect!" Will exclaimed. "She really wants to practice with me? That girl is my savior!"

Simon pushed through the door. "Savior? Who?"

115

"Abby," Will said, beaming.

Savior? Greg thought, feeling his heart plummet. *Isn't that pushing it just a little?*

Simon grinned. "You know, I've always thought Ab was a babe, but she looks *really* hot this summer." He disappeared into a shower stall and turned the water on.

"She's pretty cool too, ya know?" Will said. Then he pushed through the bathroom door and walked out.

"Yeah. Yeah, I know," Greg muttered. He hoped he wasn't making a huge mistake. Will was obviously infatuated with Abby. And Abby obviously thought she was in love with Will. What if no matter how bad she bombed, they felt some kind of crazy connection when they were alone?

Greg placed his hands on the sides of the sink, bracing his arms and staring daggers at himself in the mirror as Simon started to sing at the top of his lungs. "Good going, brainiac."

Eleven

"UGH! DAMON LETS you keep the cabin like this?" Abby wrinkled her nose at the piles of balled-up clothing and other dirty junk strewn all over the floor of Greg's room. They'd just gotten out of dinner, and Abby had come over to meet Will for their rehearsal. But Will was in the bathroom, and now Abby was hanging out in the trash heap the guys called home.

"Weird, huh?" Greg answered, sifting through a pile of doubtlessly pungent laundry next to his cot. "I think he's losing his edge. As long as it's clean for Saturday inspection, he doesn't say anything."

"Interesting. Well, you guys definitely aren't going to win the cleanest cabin award or anything." Abby stepped on a brown apple core, snatched it up, and chucked it out an open window. "So what're you going to wear on your hot date?" she asked, hoping Greg would pick up on the hint of sarcasm. It was

Tuesday night—movie night—and Abby couldn't believe he was actually taking Joanna on their date tonight, the night they were showing *Clueless*—Abby and Greg's favorite film. The two of them sometimes spent entire afternoons chowing down on microwave popcorn, debating who knew the most lines. It was like treason for him to watch it with someone else.

"I don't know," Greg said. He pulled a wrinkled long-sleeve T-shirt off the floor. "How about this?" he asked, holding it up.

Abby shook her head. "Not unless you have a washing machine and iron in your locker."

"Good point." Greg chucked the shirt over his shoulder. It landed on his muddy cleats. "But that's pretty much the problem with all my clothes. They either reek or look like I slept in them."

"Which you probably did," Abby joked.

"Nah. I sleep naked," Greg said evenly.

"*What?*" Abby screeched. She blushed so hard, she was sure that even her hair turned red.

"Kidding!" Greg said, throwing his hands up and stepping back. "Calm yourself and help me dig." He gestured at a mammoth pile of clothes under his bed.

Trying to steady the erratic pounding of her heart, Abby reluctantly lowered herself to the floor. She squatted and started picking carefully through the heap.

A huge round of cheers erupted from the other room.

"What're those guys doing in there?" Abby asked.

"Arm wrestling," Greg answered. "It's our new favorite pastime."

"I see," Abby said. Sticking too many boys in one room was definitely detrimental to their IQs.

"What about this?" Greg asked, holding out an old blue soccer tournament T-shirt. There was a tear in the seam at the top of a sleeve, and the white lettering was all faded and cracked from hundreds of washes.

"I don't think so," Abby told him, tossing aside a pair of grass-stained cotton shorts.

"Why not?" Greg asked, looking the T-shirt over. "We schooled everyone that year."

"Yeah, but Joanna doesn't know that. And isn't that shirt from, like, seventh grade? Jo won't be impressed with—" Abby stopped herself, a lightbulb suddenly turning on in her head. It was just like that time in algebra when that Pythagorean theorem thing had become crystal clear—well, sort of clear anyway.

"What?"

"You know, maybe I'm wrong," Abby said, trying to sound pensive. "Maybe you *should* wear that. You could tell Jo *all about* the tournament." Abby sat back on her heels and wrapped her arms around her knees, studying Greg as he inspected the shirt once again. It was so simple. Joanna would be thoroughly icked out by both the disheveled tee and the constant sports talk, and then she would tell Greg that she just wasn't interested. Sure, Greg might be crushed for a while, but then . . . then . . .

Then what? Abby asked herself. *He'll come running right to* you?

"I dunno," Greg was saying. He stood up and held the tattered shirt up below his chin. "Do you really think . . ."

Do you really think you could start dating Greg? Do you really think that wouldn't throw off the whole balance of the universe? Abby's brain started working overtime, and she had to block out Greg's voice in order to keep up with her thoughts. *Do you want to be with Greg? And if you do, why don't you just admit it already? Jeez! At least admit it to yourself!*

"No," Abby muttered under her breath.

"No, what?" Greg asked. "No, I shouldn't wear it, or no, it isn't heinous?"

Abby stood up and began to pace through the mess on the floor, thinking quickly. "No. Don't wear it," she said. "You at least need something clean. Something without holes. Something . . ." She walked gingerly around the room, searching for anything acceptable. If she picked something decent for him, she'd prove to that nagging little voice in her mind that she didn't want to sabotage Greg—that she wanted her friends to be happy and . . . together.

"How about this?" She grabbed a perfectly clean, only semiwrinkled blue Nike sweatshirt off someone else's bed.

"Not mine," Greg said with a shrug.

"Wear it anyway," she said adamantly. "This is important."

Suddenly desperate to just get Greg dressed and hightail it out of there, Abby started across the room without thinking to look where she was stepping. Her foot caught in the strap of someone's gym bag and her ankle twisted under her, pitching her forward. A little yelp escaped her lips as the floor rushed up at her at an alarming rate.

"Watch it!" Greg shouted.

He reached out and grabbed her, but she was too close to the floor. Greg buckled under her weight, and his knees hit the hard wood with a thud.

Before Abby had a chance to breathe, she was lying on her back, cradled in Greg's arms and looking up into his concerned green eyes. He leaned in closer, causing his bangs to fall over his eyes adorably. Abby could feel his warm breath on her cheek, and it sent goose bumps down her arms.

"Are you okay?" Greg asked in a throaty voice that wasn't his own. He smelled like peppermint and freshly cut grass.

Abby blinked. Being in Greg's arms like this was causing a pleasant, unfamiliar heady feeling, and she let it wash over her in a haze. "I don't know what's wrong with me lately," she said quietly, unable to tear her eyes away from his. "I've been such a total klutz."

Greg swallowed. "Maybe it's because you're falling in love," he whispered.

Abby's heart flopped, and she felt as if she were floating above her body. But the touch of Greg's fingers on her arms was so real, she was sure she could even feel the patterns in his fingertips.

He's going to kiss me, she realized suddenly.

He leaned in slightly, almost imperceptibly. Abby was at the same time so petrified she couldn't move and so ecstatic that she wanted to reach up and grab him herself.

Then there was a footstep near the door.

"What happened?"

Abby sprang away from Greg, her heart pounding loudly in her ears. She was overcome with fear, embarrassment, and confusion. Will was standing over her.

"Abby fell," Greg said smoothly, standing up and wiping his hands on the back of his shorts.

"Are you okay?" Will asked, offering her his hands.

"Fine," Abby managed to say. She reached, letting Will pull her up. She was trembling so hard, she didn't trust herself to stand on her own.

"Your hands are all sweaty," Will told her.

Greg shot her an unreadable glance from where he was now standing across the room. *As far away from me as possible,* Abby thought with an internal groan.

"Are they? That's weird." She stuck her hands in the pockets of her jeans and cleared her throat. "Are you, uh, ready to go?" She had to get out of there—*now.*

"Yeah. Ms. Marshall said she'd meet us at the theater. Just let me get my script," Will said slowly, looking from Abby to Greg with a questioning expression.

"I'll meet you outside," Abby blurted before Will had a chance to ask what was really going on. She wasn't even sure herself, so she didn't have a clue as to how she would respond. She could feel

Greg follow her with his eyes as she left the room, but she didn't dare look back.

"Okay, Ab," she said to herself, taking a deep, shaky breath as she burst through the door into the soothing night air. "What was *that* all about?"

"Ooooh! Look at Greg with his little flowers!" Dominic teased as the senior guys rounded the south side of Lake Emerson.

Greg managed a smile. "Shut up or I'll tell everyone about the pink stationery Jen gave you to write to her on," he shot back.

The rest of the guys laughed as Dominic's face flushed red.

Greg wiped his wet palm on his jeans, clutching the wildflowers he'd picked in his other hand. Five seconds later he started sweating all over again.

"Get a grip, Neill," he muttered to himself.

"Are you okay, man?" Simon asked, falling into step beside him. "You look a little green."

"I'm fine," Greg lied. He was so nervous, his knees were practically knocking together. "It's just a date, right?"

"Yeah, man," Simon answered, running his hand over his spiky black hair. "And we're all here to bail you out if you need it."

"Cool," Greg said.

But as they came to the big oak tree across the clearing from Joanna's cabin, Greg had to stop and take a deep breath, and he fell behind the others. He knew taking Joanna to watch a movie surrounded by a hundred other campers was not what was making him nervous. He was still freaking out about that little wrestling match with Abby back in his bunk.

If Will hadn't walked in at that moment, Greg would've done it. He would have kissed his best friend.

That was just wrong.

Greg closed his eyes, trying to forget how soft Abby had felt in his arms, how his fingertips had tingled when he'd touched her, how perfectly sweet and fresh she'd smelled. A blush rose to his cheeks.

Greg shook his head, just as he wanted to shake his thoughts right out of his mind. "This is all bad," he told himself, rapidly combing his fingers through his hair. "Joanna's waiting for you. She's beautiful, she's great, and you're going to have a terrific time."

Terrific? Who used words like that? He must really be going nuts.

"Hey, Neill!" Damon yelled over his shoulder. The guys were all standing outside Birchwood. "We're making this pit stop for you. Let's go."

Greg squared his shoulders and marched determinedly across the clearing, passing the guys without a glance. This time he ignored the high-pitched voices floating through the screen windows and rapped quickly on the door frame.

Kristen appeared almost instantaneously, wearing her normal uniform of baggy blue shorts, white T-shirt, and tattered baseball cap. "Hey there, camper," she said jovially, looking him up and down. "Nice shirt."

"Uh, thanks," Greg said, glancing down at the blue sweatshirt he'd finally decided to swipe from Dominic.

"We'll be right out," Kristen said, turning. "Joanna! Your date's here." Giggles exploded from the window section. The guys mumbled and laughed.

"Hi, Greg," Joanna said, gracing him with a demure smile.

"Hey. You look nice," Greg said awkwardly.

She was wearing a little black cotton dress and sandals and had a pair of tiny, glittering barrettes over her ears, holding back her short hair. She was showing a lot of leg, and the slim cut of the dress complimented her petite figure. Still, Greg couldn't help thinking that Abby had looked much better in *her* little black outfit. He felt his ears flare up. Now he was blatantly comparing Abby and Joanna. His train of thought was getting ugly.

"So, are those for me?" Joanna asked.

"What? Oh, right. Flowers." Greg held his makeshift bouquet out to her. One of the tall purple flowers had broken just below the bud and was swinging around limply. "I picked them this afternoon."

Joanna took the bouquet, holding it up to her nose. "That's so sweet," she said. "It's too bad we have to all walk over together. It doesn't really feel much like a date this way, does it?"

"I guess not. But it'll be fun," Greg assured her. He was actually kind of relieved to have the group. It took the pressure off a little. And he was worried

125

that if he got too much solo time with Jo, he might do something really wacked like they did in the movies—call her Abby or something by mistake.

"I'll go put these in a . . . well. . . I don't have a vase," Joanna said, laughing. "I'll try to find a really big cup. Be right back." The screen door bounced a couple of times before it closed behind her.

Greg shot a confident look at his friends for good measure, then dropped his head back to look at the stars.

I wish that Joanna and I have an incredible time tonight and that I fall completely in love with her and go back to having normal, nonweird feelings about Abby, he thought.

Out of nowhere a blast of light streaked across the sky.

Greg heard the screen door swing open behind him. "Did you see that?" Joanna asked, suddenly at his side. The rest of the girls filed out behind her. "That was a shooting star. We can make a wish."

"I already did," Greg said with a forced smile as they started down the steps. He just had a sinking feeling it wasn't going to come true.

I almost kissed Greg. I almost kissed Greg. I almost kissed Greg.

Abby was dimly aware that Will was pacing in front of her, practicing his lines, but all she could hear was her own repetitive thoughts and the pounding of her heart.

"Are you ever coming back, uh . . . Abby?"

"I'm sorry. What did you say?" Abby looked up at Will from her seated position center stage and was blinded by an intense yellow glare just to the left of his face. Ms. Marshall was up in the booth, testing the lights, and they kept blinking on and off all around Abby and Will. It was like practicing at a disco. Abby held up her right hand to shield her eyes, but all she could see was floaty purple spots.

"Where were you?" Will asked, rolling his script up like a tube.

On the floor of your cabin looking into Greg's eyes? "What do you mean?" she asked, pushing herself up off the cracked, splintery floor. "I'm right here. Never left." She stood in front of him.

Will laughed and shook his head, causing his brown locks to fall across his shoulders. "No, you're not. You were totally spaced for a second there. Are you not into this? 'Cause you don't *have* to help me if you don't want—"

"No!" Abby stated a little more loudly than she'd intended. Will looked startled. "I mean, I really want to make up for what happened Sunday." She grabbed his wrist and led him over to a big wooden box that served as a platform riser. "Sit," she said. Will complied, tucking his hair back behind his ears.

Abby settled in next to him. She *had* to help him practice. If she didn't occupy herself, she knew she'd be internally replaying her almost kiss with Greg all night. She needed to stay focused on Will and his play and on the fact that she was supposed

to have a crush on him. She could *not* keep thinking about Greg and the perfect wave of his hair and
the texture of his shirt and the taut muscles in his
arms she'd never really noticed before—

"All right. So, let's take it from 'You don't even
know what you want,'" Will said.

Abby almost laughed. He had no idea how that
line totally hit home at this moment.

She gathered her hair behind her shoulders and
sat up straight, clearing her throat. Suddenly she felt
very self-conscious. She'd never acted before. She
felt as if she were about to give an oral report in
front of the entire student body of Passmore High.

"Maybe we should stand," she said, jumping up.

"Okay," Will said, rolling his eyes slightly. He
stood and walked a few feet away from her, then
looked down at his script. "Go ahead," he murmured.

Abby smoothed down her red tank top,
searched the page until she found the line Will had
indicated, and took a deep breath. "You don't even
know what you want," she said loudly, making sure
to articulate every word. "How can *you* possibly
presume to *know* what *I* want?" She pressed her
hand to her chest and looked at Will with what she
hoped was a challenging expression.

Will just laughed. "What was that?" he gasped
out through his guffaws.

"What? I was trying to be dramatic," Abby said,
blinking innocently. All of a sudden she was very
hot. The lights were blaring down, and her eyes

were beginning to water. It would be so nice to be sitting in a cool, dark room, watching a nice romantic comedy. . . .

"Sorry," Will said, attempting to pull on a straight face. "Just . . . um . . . tone it down a little. We're running lines here, not learning to project for Broadway."

Abby's blood boiled, and not from the spotlights this time. Where did Will get off criticizing her? She was only doing this to help him. He wanted toned down? Fine. "How could you possibly presume to know what I want?" she muttered, staring down at her script.

"You don't have to give me *nothing*," Will said with a hint of exasperation. He started to pace back and forth again. The floor groaned and creaked under his heavy tread. "How am I supposed to respond to that?"

Abby stared at Will. Was he being sarcastic now? Where had that self-satisfied smirk come from? And, come to think of it, his arms now looked kind of twiggy sticking out of the short sleeves of his burgundy T-shirt.

"Try it again," Will said, turning his back on her and hunching over his script like a spoiled child.

Abby stuck her tongue out at him. "How could you possibly presume to know what I want?" she said in a normal tone of voice. She focused on the tiny pieces of yellow foam spilling out of a ripped seat in the front row and waited for his next criticism.

"I just . . . I thought . . . oh, I don't know what I thought," Will recited.

Delivered like a true De Niro, Abby thought sarcastically. At least he'd decided to get on with rehearsal. "Maybe if I go, it'll give you some time to figure it out," she read. She felt Will step closer to her.

"You're going, then?" he said in a husky voice. "Are you ever coming back?"

"That's up to you," Abby said, holding the script closer to her face. It was kind of hard to read in the harsh stage light. The words kept shifting and blurring on the page. "If you can give up your silly games. If you can change, I'll come back."

What a doormat this woman was.

"I can change. I *will* change." Will grabbed Abby's hand and she jumped. She looked down at their entwined fingers, and her heart skipped a beat. Then she felt . . . disturbed. What was he doing? "Just give me the chance to show you," he finished.

Abby quickly scanned the page until she landed on two words of stage direction.

They kiss.

This *was* the kissing scene!

"Show me? How?" Abby said uncertainly. She prayed to the theater gods that the stage would open up and swallow her—now.

Will recited his lines. Abby's eyes were riveted on the page as she followed along with the short monologue. She was acutely aware that Will's eyes were glued to her cheek and his chest seemed to be heaving slightly as he spoke. Her heart was thundering like a stampede of wild horses. She had to get out of there.

Then Will stopped talking. The silence in the theater was like a vacuum. He squeezed her hand. Abby looked into his deep brown eyes and froze.

"Should we really kiss?" he asked in a whisper.

This was it. The moment of truth was upon her. She'd been waiting for this since she'd first spotted Will and had mangled her toe in his honor.

And all Abby could think in response to his question was—*Um . . . no?*

She realized with a start that this was not what she wanted. Her heart had slowed to normal. Her breathing was perfectly fine. Her senses weren't remotely heightened. In fact, they were dulled. This was nothing like the way she'd felt earlier. The way she'd felt with . . .

Greg.

"Abby?"

Will's lips were ridiculously close to hers.

Dropping both his hand and her script at the same time, Abby backed away. "I . . . uh . . . I don't think so," she said. Her heel hit the riser, and she stumbled backward.

"Why? What'd I do?" Will asked, advancing toward her.

"Nothing!" Abby knew she was acting like a lunatic. She grasped the first excuse that popped into her mind. "I just don't feel well," she told him, realizing her stomach was actually doing a little foreboding dance. "I think I should go lie down."

"You do look like you're gonna hurl," Will said,

stopping abruptly as if he was afraid she might blow her chunks on his shoes.

Nice, Abby thought. *Very compassionate.*

"Maybe I should walk you home?" Will offered tentatively. Abby instantly felt bad for judging him too quickly. Maybe he was just unsure around sick people. Not everyone could have George Clooney's bedside manner. Will gathered up his backpack and started shoving the scripts inside.

Abby's heart twisted. All she wanted right now was to be alone so that she could sort out her feelings. But she didn't want to be harsh.

"Yeah, that would be nice," she said, wrapping her arms around herself. She'd made it to the wings of the stage, and it was decidedly cooler out from under the lights.

"Ms. Marshall, I'm gonna walk Abby back. She's not feeling well," Will shouted toward the back of the theater.

"Is she okay?" Ms. Marshall's face appeared in the lighting booth window.

"I'm fine. I just need some air," Abby answered.

"Okay. I'll see you kids tomorrow." Ms. Marshall disappeared again.

Will followed Abby out the side door and put a comforting hand on her back. Even though she felt no wild rush of emotion at his gesture, she was glad to have him supporting her.

The fact that she'd just realized she was in love with her best friend was making her feel rather faint.

Twelve

As Greg watched Cher and Josh kiss in the final moments of *Clueless* his right leg bounced up and down. He couldn't wait to get out of the jam-packed main cabin. He had never *not* enjoyed a movie so much in his life.

Joanna shifted in her seat beside him and sighed. Greg had to shut his eyes to keep from glaring at her. Her constant movement had kept the chair creaking all night and had kept Greg's nerves on edge. And she hadn't laughed *once* during the entire movie, even though she'd never seen it before. He couldn't believe that there was actually a teenage girl on the planet who hadn't seen *Clueless*. Greg had seen it more times than he could remember, and he still couldn't keep from laughing out loud during certain scenes. What was wrong with this girl?

The lights came on and the room filled with shuffling feet, chattering conversation, and a smattering of applause. Greg smiled ruefully. At least some people had appreciated it.

"Uh, what'd you think?" Greg asked Joanna. Her eyes looked a little glassy. Maybe she was just tired. Or maybe she had a rule against laughing in public.

"It was . . . interesting," Joanna commented, turning to follow the rest of the campers from their row out into the aisle.

Interesting? Greg mouthed behind her back. This was unbelievable. No. It was a travesty, that's what it was.

"You seemed to like it, though," Joanna said, glancing over her shoulder.

"It's one of my favorite movies," Greg responded as they stepped outside and caught up with the rest of their friends. Everyone else was already engrossed in their own conversations about the movie. Greg took a deep breath of the clean air and felt his shoulders relax slightly. Soon he'd be back in his cot, listening to Simon and Dominic snore in stereo, backed up by the chirping of crickets outside. He couldn't wait to get there and start thinking about—

"Are you serious?" Joanna asked, giving him an incredulous look. "So you've seen it before."

"Yeah. I mean, Abby and I watch it all the time. It's her favorite too. I'm surprised she never told you." Greg kicked at the ground while he walked. "I can't *believe* you didn't like it." A bunch of little kids playing tag ran by, followed by their counselor.

Greg half wished he could join them.

"It was okay," Joanna said, looking wounded.

Greg instantly felt like a self-centered loser. He hadn't meant to hurt her feelings. So they had different taste in movies. It wasn't like he and Abby agreed on everything either. After all, Ab's favorite TV show was *Buffy the Vampire Slayer,* which Greg just did not get. Of course, Abby always said that was because he was so unhip.

"What's your favorite movie?" Greg asked. Maybe she'd mention something else he liked.

"Well, there's *The Piano,* and *Cold Comfort Farm,* and *Sense and Sensibility.*" Joanna ticked off the films on her fingers and scrunched up her face as if she was really concentrating. "I also loved *Seven Years in Tibet*—but then, that was mainly because of Brad."

Greg nodded and smiled, but he knew he didn't look interested. He hadn't seen any of those movies. He hadn't even heard of *Cold Comfort . . .* whatever it was. It sounded like a nasal decongestant to him. He also couldn't help noticing that they were about to pass the theater—the huge, dark building in which Abby and Will were probably making out right now. With effort Greg turned his attention back to Jo and latched onto the only thing she'd mentioned that he could relate to.

"You like Brad Pitt?" he asked.

"Oh! I love him . . . ," Joanna started to gush.

An invisible force pulled Greg's eyes back to the theater. He stared at the double metal doors, as if he could somehow develop X-ray vision and find out what was going on inside.

His heart was a jumble of fear and hope. Maybe Will had called the whole thing off already, realizing that Abby couldn't act her way through an episode of *Barney*. Then again, maybe the guy had taken one look into Abby's bright blue eyes and . . . Greg shuddered.

"But I *really* liked his hair in *Legends of the Fall*. Long hair on a guy is just so . . ."

Greg was pretty sure that whatever Abby and Will were doing, neither one of them was being subjected to a chronology of Brad Pitt's hairstyles. "So, who's your favorite actress?" he interrupted, figuring talking about Claire Danes would interest him more.

Joanna started to answer, her eyes shining with excitement over her subject, but then she skidded to a halt and her jaw dropped slightly.

"I, uh . . . I . . . uh . . ."

"What's the matter?" Greg asked with genuine concern. She looked as if she'd just found out her precious Brad had shaved his head.

Out of nowhere Joanna reached up and grabbed Greg at the nape of his neck, turning him to face her. "Kiss me quick," she said, her eyes wide with desperation.

What the—

But before Greg could even finish his thought, Joanna had pulled his face to hers and locked his lips in a kiss.

Greg's arms stiffened at his sides, his eyes popping

open. Joanna's hands were locked around the back of his neck.

Why is she doing this? Greg's mind screamed.

She broke away, and her eyes darted to the right. Still gasping from confusion and shock, Greg followed her gaze. At first all he saw was the rest of the senior campers, who had stopped to chat before splitting up for the night.

But then he felt his world crumble around him.

Abby was walking along the path toward the girls' bunks with Will, ahead of the rest of the crowd. Will's arm was around her shoulders. And Abby's cheek was resting on his chest. Her eyes were even semiclosed.

As Greg's mind and heart slowly, painfully registered what he was seeing, a realization so bizarre and totally mortifying came over him that he could barely breathe.

This wasn't just a crush. He was falling in love with Abby. And not only was he falling in love with her, but he had already lost his chance—to Will.

At that very moment Abby lifted her head and looked in his direction. Before Greg could catch her eye and let her read all of the emotions and thoughts on his face, he did the only thing he could think to do.

He grabbed Joanna and kissed her.

And this time he closed his eyes.

★   ★   ★

Now Abby *really* felt like she was going to hurl.

In fact, she was pretty sure she'd never felt nausea quite this strongly before.

Greg was standing not ten yards away, wearing the shirt that *she'd* picked out for him, and he was playing tonsil hockey with her best friend.

Oh, no, Abby thought. *This is so not happening. This is undoubtedly one of those too-many-Oreos-before-bed nightmares.*

How could he possibly ignore the connection they'd made back in his cabin? Abby brought a trembling hand to her forehead. Unless he hadn't felt the connection. Unless it had all been in Abby's head. Was that even possible? Had he been leaning closer to her because his neck was weak or something?

"Abby? You're freakin' me out here." Will's voice broke through the barrage of her doubts and questions. "Are you okay?"

"Yeah, I'm fine," Abby said shakily.

"Well, you don't look fine," Will said uncertainly. He had one hand on the small of her back and one clasping her wrist, as if he was afraid she would faint if he let go.

Maybe she would faint. Her heart was fluttering dangerously, and her mind was swimming in a hazy fog. But then one thought broke through all the rest, becoming crystal clear. Her competitive nature was calling.

Two could play at this game.

"Abby?" Will's voice was low, husky, even . . . sexy.

Okay—she could do this. Taking a deep breath, Abby smiled as convincingly as possible. "How about that kiss?" she asked, tossing back her hair flirtatiously.

"But—," he said, baffled.

"But nothing," Abby returned, sounding nothing like herself, even to her own ears. She glanced around quickly to make sure no counselors were watching. The coast was clear.

Abby slid her hand around Will's neck, pulled him to her, and caught his lips with hers. Will let out a little groan of surprise before Abby felt his body relax and his warm arms wrap around her waist.

She waited for the thrilling sensation of kissing an incredibly hot guy to overcome her . . . but it didn't. What did come over her was the realization that after this moment, she'd never in her life get the chance to be this close to Greg.

And she felt a single tear slide down her cheek.

Thirteen

Greg charged down the soccer field the following morning, squinting through the light mist that was falling as he dribbled the ball in front of him. He'd woken up to a blanket of threatening clouds and thick, humid air. Even though the weather complemented his mood perfectly, it wasn't the best condition in which to play soccer.

"Cross! Cross!" Dominic shouted as he ran parallel with Greg on the opposite side of the field.

Ignoring his teammate, Greg kept his concentration trained on the ball and on the field in front of him. He could feel a defender coming up behind him to his right—he instinctively knew it was Abby. They were playing a boys-versus-girls scrimmage, and she'd been on him like a wet shirt all day. Greg was not going to give her the satisfaction of forcing him to pass.

"Neill! Cross!" Dominic yelled with obvious exasperation.

Greg glanced up for a split second, and Abby took the opportunity to kick the ball out from under him. It went scooting right over to Manisha, who promptly started up the field. Greg stopped for a moment to catch his breath and looked at Abby with a questioning expression. Why was she trying to make him look bad? She'd already taken a paper shredder to his heart.

"You snooze, you lose!" Abby said with a shrug before taking off.

Greg pushed his sweat-dampened hair off his forehead and started jogging up the field. Abby was trying a little too hard to get under his skin. She was panting, her face was all blotchy red, and her eyes were watering. She was totally overexerting herself for the sole purpose of proving that he had the talent of a pea.

"Come on, Neill! Hustle!" Logan yelled from the sidelines, clapping twice as if Greg were a dog.

Greg upped his speed a little, keeping his eyes trained on Abby's bouncing braid. He wasn't going to take this anymore. It was time for an explanation.

"Stewart!" Greg shouted. She didn't flinch. Greg full out ran. "Hey, Abby," he called, an edge in his voice. She finally slowed. "What's your problem?" he asked.

Abby turned to glare at him. "*My* problem?" she asked, her eyebrows popping up.

"Yeah, *your* problem. We're playing soccer here, not *Xena: Warrior Princess*. You've been on me all day," Greg spat. "I thought love was supposed to make people all giddy and happy, not give them violent tendencies."

Abby's eyes narrowed. They looked as stormy as the sky under her long, dark lashes. "Look, *Neill*," she said. "If you can't keep up with me, maybe you should just get off the field."

Greg felt as if he'd been punched in the gut. Abby had never spoken to him like that. He was pretty sure she'd never used that tone with anyone before in her life. "Is Will giving you attitude lessons now?" he asked shakily. He could have smacked himself for letting the wimpiness and jealousy get into his voice.

"Neill! Stewart! I've had enough!" Logan yelled. "Either get back in the game or move your butts off the field."

Startled, Greg looked up at his coach and then down at his cleats. He'd totally forgotten he was supposed to be playing soccer. The rest of the kids on the field were still playing, but they were shooting quick glances in Greg's direction, blatantly curious about the commotion.

"Now!" Logan yelled.

"Yeah, c'mon, Greg. Quit whining and try to keep up," Abby said, jogging backward.

Greg saw red. He'd always thought that was just an expression, but at that moment his anger paralyzed him. What had happened to Abby? Had Will transformed her into a wisecracking snot in one night?

Greg put his hands on his hips and started to walk toward the action. He knew that if Will showed up on the field at that moment, Greg would jump him. Will hadn't only taken Abby away before Greg had even gotten a chance to tell her how he felt, he'd also changed his best friend with one little kiss. Well, one long lingering kiss, actually, Greg recalled, his heart twisting painfully.

He was mad at Will for stealing Abby.

He was mad at Abby for changing.

He was mad at himself for ever coming to this stupid camp in the first place.

He was just plain mad.

The whistle blared, and Greg was jolted out of his thoughts. But his jaw was still set—he couldn't be jolted out of his mood.

The ball had gone out-of-bounds, and a tall girl named Patricia was about to throw it back in. Greg narrowed his eyes, feeling the adrenaline surging through his veins. *Take the ball, Abby*, he thought. *I dare you.*

The ball arced away from Patricia's fingers in seemingly slow motion. Abby stopped it with her chest, caught it with her feet, and came right at him.

Dominic was running beside Abby and he made a play for the ball, but Abby expertly blocked him out. Greg started sprinting to her, his eyes focused on the spinning ball. He couldn't even tell if she'd seen him coming, but it didn't matter—he was going to get that ball away from her. He didn't know exactly what it would prove, but he knew it would make him feel better.

The rain came down a little harder and ran down his cheeks and under the collar of his T-shirt. His feet slapped through the puddling water as he charged Abby. When he was within inches of her, he pulled back his right foot and kicked with every ounce of anger and frustration he had in him.

He slammed not only the ball but Abby's foot as well.

The ball rocketed through the rain, and one of Greg's teammates stopped it easily. Greg was already running up the field when he realized Abby had completely wiped out into the mud.

"Foul!" he heard Abby cry.

He kept running. "Cross," he yelled as he reached the goalie box.

"Coach! Foul!" Abby screeched.

"Cross!" he shouted.

His teammate saw Manisha bearing down on him and executed a perfect pass to Greg. He turned and booted it easily into the corner of the net before Lauren, the girls' goalie, even had time to blink.

All the guys cheered.

"You fouled me, Greg!" Abby shouted, stomping up to him. She was covered in mud, and her features were contorted with anger and hurt.

"That was no foul," Greg said dismissively, trying not to let her pained expression affect him.

"Why are you acting like this?" Abby choked as

tears poured from her eyes. "Why are you trying to hurt me all the time?"

"Me?" Greg asked incredulously. "You were the one who was insulting me all over the field."

And you were the one who was throwing herself all over Will in the woods last night, he thought. Greg crossed his arms over his soaking wet chest, trying to look composed. But inside, his heart was aching. He wished she would stop crying. Why did she have to cry? Why did she have to look so vulnerable that he wanted to reach out and hug her?

"I'm not talking about soccer!" Abby choked out. "God! Sometimes you are so stupid." She was racked with sobs and gasping for breath.

Greg couldn't take it anymore. He put a hand on her shoulder. "Abby, I—"

"Don't touch me!" she babbled. "I wish you'd never come here." Then she turned and ran off the field, disappearing into the woods. The skies opened up at that moment and the rain came down in sheets.

"All right, everybody! Break it up!" Kristen yelled, walking over from the sidelines with Logan. "Get your stuff. Let's get back to the cabins before we all drown."

Greg numbly followed his friends off the field.

"Greg," Kristen called, jogging up to him. He swallowed, dreading a lecture from her about what had just happened. "Watch your step," she said, eyeing him suspiciously. "If you hurt either one of

145

those girls, I'm comin' after you." Then she ran ahead, probably in an effort to catch up with Abby.

Greg felt like the mud stuck in between the spokes of his cleats. Worse. He felt like the grass that was mashed into the mud and stuck between the spokes of his cleats. In all his moaning and groaning about Abby, he'd completely neglected to consider Joanna's feelings. He'd kissed her last night—that was definitely a positive signal. And he definitely didn't have the feelings to back it up.

Greg heaved a sigh and felt his shoulders slump. If love made him treat the people he cared about like dirt, then he hoped he'd never fall in love again.

Fourteen

"AH! ISN'T THE summer just divine?" Joanna purred, stretching out lazily on her plush violet beach towel.

Stick a sock in it, Abby thought. It was their Thursday morning free period, and Joanna had suggested they spend their time sunning on the short sandy area near the lake. It had seemed like an ideal proposition at the time—a way to get away from the guys and get some serious thinking done. Joanna had been wearing a gloating expression ever since her date with Greg two nights ago, and until now Abby had done an outstanding job of avoiding the topic of The Kiss. But now that they were alone and Joanna was commenting on the wonders of the season, Abby knew it wouldn't be long before Joanna confessed her undying love for Greg.

"I don't know if divine is quite the word I would use," Abby mumbled moodily, squirting a blob of suntan lotion onto her arm. *More like disastrous,* she thought, rubbing the thick goo into her skin. As usual she'd squirted out too much, and she ended up with a visible white coating on her biceps. She ran her wrist over her arm, trying to remove some of the excess cream.

All around her other campers and counselors were flipping through magazines, writing letters, and giving each other love quizzes. Abby decided to just face the inevitable. She opened her mouth to ask Joanna about her date, but Jo started speaking before she could.

"So, how was your practice session with Will?" Joanna asked as she turned to lie on her stomach. "You haven't mentioned it at all. Was it horrible?"

"We had a great time," Abby lied, tilting her face toward the sun. It was so not fair that Joanna got to be with Greg. And for some reason Abby wanted Jo to think she was just as lucky in love. But it was still hard for her to look excited about Will. "I just don't like to kiss and tell." There. That sounded sophisticated and mysterious enough.

"Well, Greg is an amazing kisser," Joanna said, idly flipping the pages of a fashion magazine in front of her. "I bet Will kisses like a fish." She raised an eyebrow in Abby's direction.

Abby's blood turned to instant lava, and she had to dig her nails into the sand to keep from clawing Joanna. Just a couple of hours before Greg had kissed Joanna, he'd been about to kiss Abby. She was sure of it. She'd replayed the scene in her mind a million times since it had happened. Then last night, while she'd lain in bed awake, thinking about the almost kiss and the bizarre fight on the soccer field, Abby had come to the conclusion that Greg really had intended to kiss her. It hadn't been her imagination.

But it didn't make sense. If he'd *wanted* to kiss her, why had he kissed Joanna instead? Sure, Will had walked in on them, but Greg could have waited and tried again later. Was his moment with Abby just temporary insanity? *Maybe he drank the bug juice at dinner and was hallucinating that I was Joanna,* Abby thought miserably. And why had he been such a jerk to her on the field? It was all so confusing.

"Well? Does he?" Joanna asked suddenly.

"Does who what?" Abby replied, confused.

"Does Will kiss like a fish?"

Abby inhaled deeply, letting the fresh air soothe her. "He kisses just fine," Abby said lightly. "Will is a great guy. We had an incredible time at the theater, and he taught me all about technique and stage direction. He's very funny too." Wow, she was pouring the deception on thick.

"Really? What did he do?" Joanna asked, sounding interested. "I mean . . . you know I don't think he's entertaining, so I'm just . . . uh . . . curious about why you found him so amusing."

Abby curled her toes. Why did Joanna feel the need to blast Will so much? Abby should just walk away now. The aggression from yesterday's fight with Greg was flooding back to her, and she didn't want to blow up at her friend. But she also didn't understand why Jo refused to let her be happy. If Greg and Jo could have a passionate summer romance, why couldn't Abby? *Because I'm with the wrong guy,* Abby reminded herself.

"Abby, what's the matter?" Joanna asked. "You look sick." She sat up.

"I'm fine," Abby said through clenched teeth. She wished Joanna would roll over and leave her alone before she exploded for no reason. She stared out at the lake, which was filled with canoes and sailboats and campers frolicking and laughing in the water. Everyone seemed to be having fun except for her.

"No, really. You look like you're going to faint," Joanna said, pressing her hand against Abby's forehead. "You're hot."

"Of course I'm hot," Abby said evenly. "We're sitting in the sun."

"Still, maybe you should go to the infirmary. Maybe I should get Kristen. You're so pale—"

"Joanna! Would you quit it?" Abby shouted, unable to contain her irritation any longer. "You're so dramatic about everything. You sound like one of your idiotic soap operas."

Joanna gasped, and she pulled back her hand as if she'd been slapped. "Oh! So now they're idiotic?" There was a hurt expression in her eyes. "That's only my life's dream you're insulting, Abby. What's the matter with you lately?"

"I don't know," Abby responded gruffly. "Maybe I'm just confused because everyone around me is acting all psycho."

"Whatever," Joanna said, rolling her eyes. She

pulled her Walkman out of her backpack and put on the headphones. "Wake me when you've calmed down." Joanna turned the volume up loud enough for Abby to hear the bass and rolled over on her side so that Abby was staring at her back.

Abby flopped back onto her towel, and a sharp rock struck her hip. She reached under the towel, grabbed the offending rock, and flung it into the water with all her might. Her chest was heaving with anger. She couldn't believe this. What was wrong with everyone? This was supposed to be the best summer of her life, and she was getting into daily battles with her two best friends. She'd never really fought with either of them before—aside from the time Greg had beheaded her favorite doll when they were eight years old.

One thing was for sure, Abby couldn't sit still any longer. She had to get up, get away from Joanna, and get some exercise to release this aggression. She pulled the lavender peasant shirt she used as a cover-up over her head, then yanked on her denim shorts and sneakers. Tossing her stuff in her backpack, she cast one last look at Joanna's back and sighed. She'd known that remark about soaps would upset her. Forget about everyone else; Abby had been dispensing some bad attitude herself.

As she walked away from the lake area and toward the trails that led into the woods one thing was on her mind—getting things back to normal. She'd have to apologize to Joanna, and she'd have to figure out a way to get up the guts to talk to Greg again. She couldn't lose him just because every ounce of her being wanted to kiss him.

"You wanna just shoot around or do you wanna go full out one-on-one?" Will asked, dribbling a basketball along the dirt trail as he walked. They were heading for the outdoor basketball hoops outside the main cabin.

"Full out, man," Greg answered, pulling a baseball cap on backward over his hair to hold it back. "I need a good workout." What he really needed was to kick Will's butt in a legal fashion. That seemed like a valid activity for a free period.

"Maybe some of the other guys'll come over and we can get a game going," Will said.

"Nah. I'd really rather play one-on-one," Greg told him. "I'm just in the mood."

"Sure, man, whatever," Will responded. He smacked at the bushes with his hand as he shuffled along. "So, um, how was your date with Joanna the other night anyway? You haven't said much about it."

That's 'cause there's nothing to say, Greg thought. But to Will he said, "It was unbelievable." At least it wasn't a lie. He was still reeling over the fact that Joanna had kissed him. He couldn't figure out why she'd done it. At this point he didn't even really *like* the girl. They had nothing in common, and he was beginning to think she was kind of a snob.

Ever since that night and his fight with Abby the following morning, the meals in the mess hall had been strangely silent, with only detached polite conversation between the four of them. And everyone would bolt as soon as the dishes were stashed. It was pretty obvious to Greg that no one wanted to talk to anyone else about what they had all witnessed and done on Tuesday night. And Greg *still* didn't want to talk about it.

"Well, Abby's just . . . she's just beautiful," Will said with a wistful smile. "And man, can that girl kiss."

Greg's stomach turned. "Really?" Oh, how he wanted to flatten Will.

"Totally," Will answered, starting to dribble the ball again. "She must've had a lot of boyfriends."

"What's that supposed to mean?" Greg demanded defensively. Was he trying to say that Abby was easy?

"Just that she must've had a lot of practice kissing to kiss that good," Will said, his eyes concentrating on the ball as he bounced it from one hand to the other.

Greg focused on the ground as he walked to keep himself from exploding. As far as he knew, the only guy Abby had ever kissed for real was Derek Washington. They'd all gotten really silly at Greg's fifteenth birthday party and played spin the bottle. Abby had confided to him later that Derek had kissed her with tongue. She'd had to tackle Greg to the ground to keep him from going over to Washington's house to pummel the guy. Had she kissed other guys since then and not told him?

An icky, nervous, jealous feeling was beginning to seep its way from Greg's heart throughout his body. Even his legs felt heavier.

"And she sure smells good too," Will was saying.

"Can we not talk about Abby anymore?" Greg blurted as they reached the basketball court. It was so unfair. Why did this loser that had just walked into their lives get to kiss Abby and he couldn't?

"Sorry, man," Will said. "You didn't have something going with her back home, did you?"

"No," Greg said. *And thanks to you, I never will.* "She's just my friend, and I don't want to talk about her like that."

"Sure. I hear ya."

Greg walked over to the grassy area to the side of the asphalt court and dropped to the ground to tighten the laces on his high-tops. He wished he'd gotten up the guts to talk to Abby and apologize to her for their argument on the field. He'd been so afraid she'd just turn her back on him that he hadn't been able to face her. But maybe if they'd had a chance to talk things out, he wouldn't have this hollow ache where his heart used to be.

Greg untied one shoe and went to tie it again, his hands shaking. It was so bizarre that Abby was making him feel this way. For the first time in his life he really realized how beautiful and special she was. She was so talented, and she was becoming more and more strong willed and self-confident. Maybe it was because here at camp, Abby was really in her element. Greg couldn't put her out of his mind no matter how hard he tried.

Maybe it's time to stop trying, he told himself firmly, tying his lace quickly. If she wanted to be with Will this summer, fine. But he wasn't going to completely lose her over it. He had to apologize for that petty fight. He had to figure out a way to save their friendship. After all they'd been through together, he figured he owed her at least that much.

"You ready, man?" Will asked. He twirled the ball between two fingers.

Greg stood up. "I, uh, I changed my mind," he said, placing his hands on his hips. "I think I'm gonna go for a hike instead."

Will gave him a confused look. "Whatever's good for you," he said, shrugging. Then he turned and shot at the hoop. The ball slammed into the backboard and boomeranged at Will, slamming him in the chest. A couple of younger guys on the next court laughed. Greg smirked. At least he knew for sure that he could have schooled the guy. What he was about to do was more important.

He was going to think of a way to win Abby back, at least as a friend, before this whole camp thing was over.

Abby trudged her way along the hiking trail, looking for a nice clearing to stop at—someplace where she could sit down, listen to the birds and the rustling leaves, and figure out what to do next. So far the walk had helped clear her head and release the residue of her anger. Now she was left with a sort of heavy resignation. She was going to have to apologize to Greg, hope he'd agree to remain friends with her, and accept the fact that their relationship would never be the same again. She was never going to be able to look at him without feeling the magnitude of what she'd lost.

Looking down at her watch, Abby realized she'd been hiking for almost half an hour. She'd have to be heading back pretty soon if she was going to make lunch on time. She lifted the thick blanket of hair off her neck, trying to cool off as she walked along a small stream, around a bend in the trail. Suddenly she saw a flash of white out of the corner of her eye. She came to an abrupt stop at the edge of a clearing to get a closer look.

Abby's heart sped up, and she held her breath. Greg was walking into the clearing from the opposite side, and he hadn't spotted her yet. What was he doing here?

Abby had an overwhelming urge to flee before he looked up, but she knew she would never make it to a good hiding place before he saw her.

This was it. She was trapped.

"Hey," she said.

He jumped slightly and looked up, obviously startled. "Hey," he said awkwardly, looking behind him as if he was assessing his own escape route.

Abby stood only half facing him, prepared to bolt at any moment.

"What's up?" Greg asked, frozen in place.

"Not much," Abby answered. Her heart was pounding painfully now, and her hands were clammy. She'd never felt this awkward with a guy before—and she couldn't believe the guy was Greg.

"I was just . . . uh . . . just walking," Greg said, rubbing the back of his neck and taking a few steps into the clearing.

"Yeah. I guessed," Abby said with a smile, glad someone had moved. She relaxed her stance.

Greg scowled for a second but then looked at her face and seemed to realize she was just joking and not mocking him. His shoulders lowered slightly, and he smiled back at her.

It was now or never. Abby took a deep breath, closed her eyes, and spoke. "Greg, about the other day—"

"I know. I'm really sorry," he interrupted.

"*I'm* sorry," Abby returned. "I was acting like a jerk."

"*I* was the jerk," Greg said. He crossed in front of her and sat down near the stream on a large, flat rock. "I can't believe I didn't stop to see if you were okay when you tripped," he said.

"Well, maybe we were both jerks," Abby offered. She sank down next to him, picked up a stick, and started doodling in the dirt at her feet, purposely averting her eyes so that he wouldn't be able to read what she was feeling.

"Sounds fair," Greg said, laughing slightly. "You wanna shake on it?"

Abby tilted her head and looked at him. Her ponytail tumbled over her leg and tickled her skin. She seemed to be feeling everything more intensely in Greg's presence.

"Sure," she said, holding out her hand. Greg clasped her hand in his, and Abby felt his touch everywhere. Talk about intense. She withdrew quickly and wrapped her arms around her legs, staring at the ground in front of her. All she wanted to do was ask him about his date with Joanna, but it was also exactly what she *didn't* want to do. She didn't know if she could handle hearing how great it was from his own lips.

"Can I ask you a question?" she asked, stalling. She watched an ant try to struggle its way over a rock and wondered why it hadn't just walked around. That would've been so much easier.

"Yeah," Greg said, sounding wary.

Don't do it, Ab! her brain yelled.

"How was your date with Joanna?" The ant made it over the rock and scurried off.

Greg was silent. Abby started to freak out in her thoughts. Maybe he didn't want to talk about it because he didn't feel close to her anymore. Maybe their fight the other day really *had* changed everything. She felt as if her world were caving in on her.

Finally Greg shifted, sitting up straight. "It was . . . okay," he said slowly.

"Just okay?" Abby asked, almost unwilling to hope she'd heard correctly. He didn't sound thrilled.

"Yeah, well, I didn't want to say anything 'cause she's your friend and all—"

"No! Go ahead," Abby prodded, perking up considerably. This sounded almost foreboding.

"Well, to be honest," Greg began, staring out at the distance and squinting as though he was choosing his words with extreme care, "Jo and I have nothing in common. She hated the flick, and she was gushing about all these movies I'd never even heard of. She must've checked her hair in her little mirror, like, a hundred times, and she kept asking me all these really deep questions about *Clueless,* like she was analyzing *War and Peace* or something." Greg paused to take a breath and looked Abby in the eye. "To be honest, I don't even know what *you* see in her."

Abby's eyes widened. She was so positively ecstatic, she felt like laughing out loud. Greg wasn't in love with Joanna! He didn't even *like* her!

"Sorry. You're mad at me again, huh?" Greg asked, his brow furrowed with concern.

That was it. Abby burst out laughing, unable to hold it in any longer. All the emotions she'd been feeling over the past few days rushed out immediately.

"What's so funny?" Greg asked, sounding perplexed.

That only made Abby laugh harder. Her eyes were tearing, and when she looked up at Greg, he was all blurry. "That was one of the funniest things I've ever heard!" Abby exclaimed, wiping at her eyes.

Greg looked totally baffled. "You are a strange girl, Ab," he said, smiling and shaking his head.

"Thanks," Abby replied, clearing her throat as she gained control of herself. There was still one question on her mind. She'd seen Greg grab Joanna's shoulders and pull her in for a kiss. Why had he done that if he was so turned off?

Abby kicked at the dirt with the toe of her sneaker and dug a little hole, getting ready to speak. But Greg spoke first.

"And she's not even a very good kisser," he said.

"She's not?" Abby squeaked. Her toe was digging like crazy now.

Greg grunted. "It was, like, totally stiff. Like kissing one of my sisters."

"Are you serious?" Abby giggled. If Joanna heard them discussing her like this, she'd never talk to either one of them again.

"Totally," Greg answered, nodding vigorously. "Or worse." He hesitated, his eyes trained on the ground. "Like kissing you."

That caused Abby to pause.

"And how, may I ask, do you know what it's like to kiss me?" she asked finally, a challenge in her eyes.

"Oh, I've heard things," Greg said teasingly. His ears were a brighter red than she'd ever seen them before.

"From who?" Abby demanded, turning to face him head-on. Their knees touched, and she felt an electric current rush up her spine. She almost shivered.

"Come on, Ab. How many guys have you kissed?" Greg asked, looking her in the eyes. He was blushing all over now.

"So it was Will," Abby stated. "What did he say?"

"First answer *my* question, ugly," Greg said, purposely knocking her knee with his.

Abby pushed back a little. "What question, loser?" she asked.

"How many guys have you kissed?" Greg asked again. There was just a touch of trepidation in his voice.

"Exactly two," Abby answered. "You know that." She playfully pushed his shoulder.

"I was beginning to wonder," Greg said, looking down at his high-tops.

What was that supposed to mean? Abby wondered. "What? You think I'm lying to you now?" she asked, knocking his knees with her own, a little harder than he had.

"No," he said, bracing his feet and pushing back.

"Quit it." Abby laughed, shoving both his shoulders back.

"Quit what?" He jovially grasped her ponytail and whipped it into her face.

It hit her open eye and stung. "Ow! Greg!" She bodychecked him with her shoulder, throwing him off balance. He had to place his hand on the ground to keep from sprawling in the dirt. Greg glanced down at his hand, then up at Abby with a grin. "Don't you dare," she said.

Greg lunged and wiped his dirty hand on her face. Abby tried to fend him off, but she couldn't. She could feel the dirty streak on her left cheek.

"You're toast!" she shouted, laughing uncontrollably. She wrapped her arms around his waist and tackled him to the ground. She attempted to pin him like she had a hundred times before, but her knee hit a rock and she flinched, giving him a momentary window of opportunity.

Greg reached up and grabbed her wrists, circling them with his fingers like handcuffs. Abby hated it when he did this. It always made her feel helpless, and he knew it. She struggled to her knees.

"You give?" Greg asked breathlessly.

"No way," she said, her eyes flashing as she squirmed. Greg pulled himself up and knelt in front of her, smiling in satisfaction while she writhed.

Finally Abby got fed up and threw herself on top of him. Greg released her wrists in surprise and caught her in his arms as they went tumbling over. When they stopped rolling, Abby opened her eyes and froze. It was like déjà vu. Greg's face was inches from hers. His eyelids looked heavy, and his breath came in shallow bursts.

Abby could hardly breathe herself. All she could do was hope. *Please let him do it this time.*

"You give?" Greg asked in a whisper. He reached up and trailed a finger down her cheek, right along the streak he'd put there a moment before.

Abby couldn't speak. Her heart was in her throat. She just nodded, her eyes glued to his.

Slowly—agonizingly slowly—Greg lowered his mouth to hers. The moment their lips touched, Abby felt as if she were melting into him. She closed her eyes, overwhelmed by the absolute perfection of his tender lips, his delicate touch, the complete purity of the moment. She was kissing her best friend. The guy who knew her better than anyone. The guy, she was now certain, she would always love more than anyone. Her heart was so full, she felt tears of happiness fill her eyes. She squeezed them shut even tighter as Greg deepened the kiss.

Abby shakily placed her right hand on the back of his neck. Her palm grazed his ear, and she giggled. It was burning hot.

Greg broke off the kiss, and her eyes fluttered open. His green eyes were shining with contentment. "Why are you laughing?" he asked.

Abby bit her lip for a moment. "I just love you," she said happily.

Greg hesitated for an instant, a breath catching in his throat. Abby could practically feel his pulse accelerate. "I love you too, Abby," he said quietly. He lowered his lips to hers once more, but Abby placed a finger over his mouth.

"Wait," she said. "I don't kiss like one of your sisters, do I?"

"Hardly," Greg answered. "And don't bring them into this. It kills the mood."

Abby laughed. He kissed her again, and she touched his cheek with her fingertips. She knew his face as well as she knew her own, but she wanted to make sure every tactile detail of this moment was engraved on her memory forever—from the tickle of his bangs grazing her forehead to the little stick that was pressed into the back of her thigh.

Greg broke away and plucked a leaf out of her hair, holding it up to show her.

"See," he said with a heart-stopping grin. "Rolling around in the dirt *can* be romantic."

Fifteen

GREG WRAPPED HIS arms around Abby's waist and kissed her nose. She giggled and smiled up at him, causing his heart to flip-flop in his chest. It had been a little over a week since they'd first kissed, and in that time Greg had been totally tuned in to her every move. All the little things Abby had always done now had such a pulse-quickening effect on him. He couldn't get enough of her.

"Aren't you glad we were promoted to stage managers?" Abby asked, cuddling closer to him.

"Yeah. It's just too bad it's almost over," Greg said, glancing at the stage. He and Abby were standing in the wings on the night of the performance, and they weren't paying any attention to the play. Last Thursday afternoon Ms. Marshall had made them stage managers—that way they didn't have to touch anything. All they'd had to do was tell the actors when to get ready to go onstage. Now that Will and Joanna were performing the final scene, Greg and Abby didn't have any responsibilities for the rest of the night. And it was wonderfully dark and cozy in the wings when everyone else's attention was trained on the stage.

"Do you think we did the right thing? I mean, not telling them?" Abby asked.

"You wouldn't have wanted to be responsible for breaking Will's concentration again, would you?" Greg teased. They'd decided not to tell Will and Joanna about their new couple status because they were afraid Jo and Will would get angry, making the living situation for the duration of camp rather uncomfortable. Over the past week Greg had managed to avoid being alone with Joanna, just as Abby had steered clear of Will. But it had gotten extremely hard for both Greg and Abby to hide their feelings. So they'd decided they'd let their secret out *after* the play—to ensure that they didn't ruin Will and Jo's concentration.

"It's so bizarre," Abby said quietly, reaching up to fiddle with the buttons on Greg's plaid shirt. "We've hugged about a zillion times in our lives. Why does it feel so cool now?"

"Well, I've been workin' out," Greg said, flexing his biceps comically.

Abby laughed. "No! You know what I mean. You and me? A couple? Imagine what everyone at home is going to say."

"Well, all our friends will say, 'We told you so,' and your mom will probably throw us a party,"

Greg said, tucking a stray hair behind her ear. She was wearing it loose and shiny, the waves framing her face in perfection.

"In that case I'll have to borrow some more clothes from Jo," Abby said, stepping back and holding out her arms. She looked down at her sapphire-colored, long-sleeve T-shirt and khaki skirt.

Greg thought she looked gorgeous. She looked like Abby—the girl he loved—and always had. "Just wear that," he said, smiling as he grabbed her wrist and pulled her to him. "You're perfect." Abby blushed, and Greg leaned in to kiss her, thinking how strange it was to be talking mush to his best friend.

"You know what?" Abby said when they parted. Greg's heart was pounding from the kiss. He wondered if his breathing would ever be normal when he was close to Abby again. If this was what he was going to be like around her, she'd kick his butt on the soccer field every time they played.

"What?" he asked.

She entwined his fingers with hers. "Let's promise that we will never, ever become one of those annoying, lovey-dovey couples that, like, feeds each other in public."

"You read my mind," Greg said. "As long as we can be as stupid as we want in private."

Abby squeezed his hand. "Deal," she said.

"How can you possibly presume to know what I want?" Joanna's voice carried from the stage.

"Oh, my gosh!" Abby gasped, her eyes widening. "This is it!"

"This is what?" Greg asked, confused.

"The scene! It's almost over! They're gonna have to kiss soon!" Abby sounded horrified and looked amused at the same time.

"This oughta be good," Greg said. He grinned and tugged on her arm, tiptoeing toward the stage. There were a bunch of set people and other cast members packed into the wings just out of the audience's view. They were all obviously drawn there for the same reason—to see Will and Joanna finally suck face.

"They never practiced it," Abby whispered as Greg pushed their way to the front of the crowd.

"I know," Greg returned. "I can't wait. Joanna's probably gonna barf on his shoes."

"And Will's gonna feel like he's kissing his sister," Abby said dryly. Greg laughed.

They peeked out onto the stage, trying to stay far enough back so that the audience couldn't see them. Will paced as Joanna delivered her lines.

"So, we'll tell them at the cast party?" Abby whispered so softly, Greg could barely hear her.

He leaned down and pressed his cheek to hers. "Right. They can't kill us in a public place," he whispered back.

"You obviously don't know Joanna that well," Abby said. She bit her lip as she followed the action on the stage with her eyes.

"Will is gonna be devastated," Greg said with a smile. "He lost *you* after all."

"Nah. He didn't lose me. He never had me,"

Abby said. "I was always yours. We just didn't know it."

Greg chuckled. Abby maneuvered herself in front of him and leaned back into his chest. He wrapped his arms around her from behind and rested his chin on top of her head. They fit together so perfectly. It was like curling up with his favorite blanket.

"Besides, Joanna's the one who's going to be upset," Abby said seriously. "I just hope she doesn't get so mad that she decides to never speak to me again."

"Don't worry, Ab," Greg said, giving her a quick squeeze for reassurance. "It'll be fine."

"Shhh! Here it comes," Abby whispered.

Greg waited to see signs of disgust and loathing on Joanna's face as Will wrapped one arm around her and pulled her to him. But there weren't any. Jo actually looked a little nervous and excited. He could even tell that she was blushing violently under her heavy makeup.

"Either the stage lights are really hot or she's an excellent actress," Greg murmured.

"Come on, you guys," Abby urged them on quietly. "Just get it over with, and you'll never have to look at each other again."

Will slowly pressed his lips to Joanna's. She hugged her arm around his back, and Greg noticed her hands were trembling. Her knees even seemed to give a little.

"She is *good*," Greg said.

The audience erupted into wild applause as the curtain fell.

"Yes! She didn't puke!" Abby cheered loudly.

Everyone in the wings was clapping and whistling and hugging one another. Abby threw her arms around Greg, jumping up and down in excitement. "They did it! They did it! They did it!" she squealed.

"Um . . . Ab?" Greg said, releasing her as he stared at the stage.

"Yeah?" She pulled back to look at his face.

"They're still doing it."

Abby's brow wrinkled, and she whirled around to look at Joanna and Will. "Oh, my gosh!" she gasped.

Greg laughed. Will and Joanna were locked in a passionate embrace, and they hadn't come up for air once. The curtain lifted so the cast could come out and take their bows, and Will and Joanna were *still* kissing.

Finally Joanna seemed to notice the cheering and broke away, totally flushed. Will was grinning like a fool, and his eyes were all glazed.

"Jeez! He looks like he's gonna fall over!" Abby exclaimed.

"I think Will got a very different kiss than I did," Greg commented.

Abby smacked him on the chest with the back of her hand. "Try never to mention that you kissed my best friend before you kissed me," Abby warned.

"I thought I *was* your best friend," Greg said in mock confusion.

"You know what I mean." Abby laughed and looked back at the stage, shaking her head in wonder.

Greg slipped his arm around her and watched as Joanna and Will held hands and bowed together. When they stepped back to let the curtain drop again, Will whispered in Joanna's ear. She laughed the most natural laugh Greg had ever heard from her lips, and she stood on her toes to kiss Will on the cheek.

"How did *this* happen?" Abby asked, running her hand through her hair.

"I don't know," Greg answered. "But I have a feeling telling them about us won't be as hard as we expected."

"What is he *doing?*" Joanna wailed through her laughter, covering her face with both hands.

Abby patted Joanna on the back sympathetically. "You got the weird one, Jo. That's for sure," she said.

Will was in the center of a crowd of people on the dance floor, shaking his hips and twirling a string of Mardi Gras beads over his head. After the play all the campers had adjourned to the main cabin for a wrap-up party, and one thing had become clear since the music had started—Will Stevenson was a dancing machine.

Abby and Joanna laughed as Will grabbed Babs

and started tangoing with her across the wooden floor. Abby was still baffled over the fact that Joanna and Will seemed to have fallen instantly in love, but on the walk over here Joanna had insisted it wasn't instantaneous, she'd just been in denial.

I can relate to that, Abby thought, watching Greg weave his way toward them, balancing three cups of punch. Joanna just had a more emphatic and sarcastic method of denying her feelings than Abby did.

"Listen, Jo," Abby began, "I never apologized for the way I acted at the lake last week. I was just all freaked out about you and Greg." She and Joanna had both acted like the little scene had never happened, but it had been bothering Abby for days.

"Don't worry about it," Joanna said. "I *completely* understand." Her eyes twinkled knowingly.

She must have been feeling the same way, Abby thought.

"Ladies," Greg said, bowing his head slightly as he handed them their drinks. "I'm afraid our friend Will here is in need of a straitjacket."

"Woo!" Will called out at the top of his lungs. He was now doing a John Travolta–style twist in the middle of the makeshift dance floor. Every single pair of eyes in the room was trained on him.

Joanna let out a burst of laughter. "He's not a mental case. I just have that effect on guys," she said, watching Will with an infatuated expression.

Abby shot Greg a look and giggled. He rolled his eyes back in his head and stuck out his tongue comically, making little choking sounds.

"Oh, grow up, Greg," Joanna scolded.

"He doesn't have to grow up," Abby said, stepping in front of Greg defensively. "He's just fine the way he is." Sooner or later she was going to have to apologize for making him feel unsophisticated in the art room the other day. He was, without a doubt, *much* cooler than Will.

Will tangoed himself over to Joanna and executed a little twirl in front of her. But when he smiled at her, he almost looked shy. "May I have the honor of this dance?"

"I thought you'd never ask," Joanna said demurely, holding out her hand to him. Will grinned and pulled Joanna onto the dance floor.

"Cheesy!" Abby and Greg called out together.

Abby grinned and sipped her punch. She couldn't have asked for a more perfect atmosphere to match her mood. The main cabin was decorated with red, white, and pink streamers in honor of the love theme of the play. There were heart-shaped Mylar balloons tied to the chairs, and red balloons floated all over the dance floor. It was like Valentine's Day in the middle of the summer. And in the true spirit of Cupid, she and Greg had found love right under their noses, Joanna and Will had fought their way into the beginning of a relationship, and even Kristen and Damon seemed to be getting along rather well, flirting over at a table in the corner. Abby made a mental note to ask Kristen about that later.

Greg smacked his empty cup down on the table, then snatched Abby's from her and did the same. "I feel the need to boogie!" he said, grabbing her wrist.

"Boogie?" Abby repeated. Okay, *everyone* had gone insane.

"Yes. Boogie," he shouted over the music, pulling her toward the dance floor. "But don't tell anyone I said that," he called over his shoulder.

"I wouldn't dare," Abby said, flashing him a conspiratorial smile as she faced him on the dance floor.

Greg took one look at her expression and frowned. "Hey! If you're my girlfriend, you can't mock me anymore."

"Are you kidding?" Abby asked. "Where's the fun in the relationship if we're not allowed to trash each other?"

Greg scratched the back of his head and appeared to be considering her words.

"Good point," he said finally. "Let's dance."

"Hey! You guys!" Will and Joanna came dancing over and waltzed right in between Abby and Greg. "We just got an idea," Will said, stopping to catch his breath. The boy had been working out so hard all night, he looked like he'd just run a mile.

Abby smiled. "What's up?" she asked as Greg wrapped his arm around her casually.

"We should all come back as CITs next year!" Joanna squealed, grasping Abby's arm. "It would be so cool! The four of us—together again."

"Only then we'd have power," Greg said slyly.

"Yeah. And I won't kiss your girl if you don't kiss mine," Will said, chucking his chin in Greg's direction.

Abby felt herself blush. "Why don't we forget all of that ever happened," she said. She knew they'd just make each other feel nonstop uncomfortable if they kept bringing up their couple-swapping adventure.

"I'm all for that," Joanna agreed. "And . . . ," she said, poking Will on the chest. "We are not *your girls*. We don't belong to anyone." She smacked him in the stomach with the back of her hand.

"Great," he said, rubbing his abdomen. "She's a feminist too."

Abby laughed and tossed her hair behind her shoulder. "I'll agree to come back on one condition," she said. "We all make a pact not to let any of our campers date."

"Deal," the others said emphatically. Abby laughed again.

"Let's shake on it," Greg said, reaching out a hand to Will. Will hesitated a split second before shaking Greg's hand, but as they sealed the deal both guys grinned.

Abby knew there would be no hard feelings between them over her and Joanna. She reached over and hugged Jo, happy that everything had turned out so well for her friend—even if she was probably in for the most melodramatic relationship ever. Hey! The girl thrived on drama.

A slow song started up, and Abby released Joanna.

"Sorry, Jo," she said. "I'd rather dance this one with *my* man."

Will laughed. "You better watch out, Neill," he said to Greg jovially. "She's scary."

"Just the way I like her," Greg said, pulling Abby close and tucking his hand under her hair to tickle her neck. Abby's heart felt as if it were skipping every third beat. When Greg wrapped his arms around her and started to sway to the music, she let the warmth of his embrace consume her. She rested her cheek against his chest, listening to the beat of his heart and letting the rest of the world fade away.

"Hey. This is our first dance as a couple," Greg whispered.

"I guess that makes this our song," Abby said, tilting her head back to look into his eyes.

Greg smiled and kissed her softly on the lips. "I thought 'Old MacDonald' was our song," he teased.

Abby smiled as she remembered the videotape Greg's parents had of the two of them singing "Old MacDonald" together in a talent show when they were six years old. It suddenly struck her just how long she and Greg had been friends. They had no real secrets. After all these years, what had made them fall in love?

"What're you thinking?" Greg asked as they moved ever so slightly to the music.

"I was wondering how we ended up here," Abby said, gazing up at him.

"That's easy," Greg said. "You dragged me here."

"No, stupid," Abby joked, rolling her eyes. "I mean here—together—as in, a couple."

"I don't know about you," Greg said. He lifted her off the ground and twirled her around in a circle. Abby laughed as he replaced her on the floor. "But I'm here because of Will."

"Will made a convincing argument about our relationship?" Abby asked, looking surprised.

"He made an incredible argument," Greg said matter-of-factly. "He tried to take you away. And I didn't like it."

Abby recalled with sudden clarity the way she had felt when she'd seen Joanna entwined in Greg's arms. "I didn't like it either," she agreed.

"Okay, so let's make one more pact," Greg said, touching his forehead to hers. He clasped both her hands in his and held them down at their sides.

"Let's promise we'll never let anyone steal us away from each other again," Abby offered with a smile.

"You read my mind," Greg said.

"Well, when you put your head right up against mine, it's not that hard," Abby told him, laughing. "So? You promise?"

"I promise," Greg answered huskily.

Abby held her breath. Greg leaned over slowly, teasingly, then finally pressed his lips to hers. Abby felt a rush of warmth, excitement, and comfort as she pulled him closer. His kiss was still new, but somehow familiar. She felt as if their hearts were bound to each other by all they'd been through together and all they were yet to experience. She had an overwhelming sense that she was exactly where she was meant to be.

When they parted, Greg pressed his forehead to hers again and looked directly into her eyes. "Hey, Stewart," he said with a grin. "Why didn't we think of this sooner?"

"Beats me," Abby returned, her heart pounding against her rib cage as she returned his smile. "But I'm sure looking forward to making up for lost time."

Do you ever wonder about falling in love? About members of the opposite sex? Do you need a little friendly advice but have no one to turn to? Well, that's where we come in . . . Jenny and Jake. Send us those questions you're dying to ask, and we'll give you the straight scoop on life and love in the nineties.

DEAR JAKE

Q: *I want to tell Miles that I like him, but we have a lot of the same friends and they're always around when we're together. I really don't want everyone to know how I feel. How can I get him alone so that we can talk privately?*

EV, Phoenix, AZ

A: It's tough when you fall for one of the members of your gang, and you have to find a way to let him know without broadcasting the news to the whole group. I usually advocate doing these things face-to-face so that you can watch his expression and judge the body language. However, in your case I'd say that a phone call might be more effective. Give Miles a ring and ask if he'd like to catch a movie or grab a bite to eat alone together. If he says okay, be casual at first, then once you're with him, open up about your feelings.

Q: My friend Kimberly told me that all good-looking guys are players. My boyfriend, Doug, is gorgeous, so she thinks I should break up with him before he hurts me. Should I listen to her?

NJ, Queens, NY

A: Okay, this is one of the easiest questions I've ever been faced with: *No,* you should not by any means listen to anything this silly friend of yours tells you. Let me guess, Kimberly also informed you that the best way to get a guy is to pretend to be someone totally different from yourself and other false tales. Or maybe Kimberly isn't just ignorant—it's possible that she's actually being sly and angling to snag your boyfriend for herself once you set him free. Whatever the explanation, be wary of things that come out of your friend's mouth. Players come in all shapes and forms, and whether a guy is attractive or not has no connection to how he'll treat you. As long as you're happy with your boyfriend and have no reason to be suspicious, hang on to him.

Q: My good friend Dan is always complaining to me about his relationship with his girlfriend. I've had a secret crush on him for a long time, but I never wanted to get in the way of things between him and Sara. I think cheating is totally wrong, and plus I even like Sara. But I can't help feeling *like they're just not right for each other, while Dan and I are so in sync. Is it okay to tell Dan how I feel?*

PY, Pelzer, SC

A: It's hard to understand a relationship from the outside; a lot of couples fight all the time but are still fiercely devoted to each other. If you spill your feelings to Dan, it might make things between you tense, as well as strain your interactions with Sara. However, if it's getting to the point where you can't deal with hearing one more speech starting out, "Listen to what Sara did this time . . . ," go ahead and bring it up. Start off by asking him how much he really wants to maintain the relationship he's in. Assure him that you want him to be happy, and if he is, then you'll drop it and never bring it up again. Then if he admits that he's been thinking of ending it with Sara, you can tell him that you've had thoughts about the two of you. . . .

DEAR JENNY

Q: *I'm pretty popular in my school, and I get asked out a lot. None of the guys I've dated have ever interested me too much, though. Recently I realized that I really like hanging around this guy Mark, but he's not popular at all, and I'm* worried that if I went out with him, my reputation would go down the drain. Yeah, it sounds superficial, but I can't help feeling like I'm just too good for Mark—could he really make me happy?

CW, Appleton, ME

A: It doesn't just *sound* superficial; if you reject this guy because of his status when you have genuine feelings for him, I'd worry about you. Here's a quick lesson from someone who's been around and back: Once you find someone who makes your heart jump and your palms sweat, grab him and don't let go. If you let everyone else's opinions dictate who you date, you'll never be content. People—including you—will soon forget that he's supposed to be unpopular when they see the two of you having a great time and making each other totally happy.

Q: *My boyfriend, Paul, is great. I only wish that he would compliment me more often. I've asked him about it, and he tells me that he loves me and thinks I'm beautiful, but he just isn't the type of guy to say it all the time. Is there anything I can do to make him more sensitive?*

KM, Locust Grove, VA

A: Other than a brain transplant, I know of few options that can turn a reticent guy like Paul into a smooth talker with flowery praise sliding off his tongue. However, this doesn't have to be a bad thing—I've known guys who can say things that melt my heart and then they turn around and break it. I've also known shy guys who can barely squeeze out the words, "Yeah, you, uh, look nice tonight," but are total sweethearts.

If it's really bothering you a lot, ask Paul if he can compromise and just *try* to say some nice things more frequently. Promise him that you'll make an effort in return to accept him as he is.

Q: *Sean is the love of my life, I'm sure of it. None of the guys I've been with in the past mean anything to me anymore, but I am still friends with a couple of ex-boyfriends. However, Sean doesn't want me to hang around them because he gets really jealous. I was angry until I realized that I really don't want him talking to his ex-girlfriends either. How can we resolve this?*

LA. Randallstown, MD

A: The world of ex-loves is complex; often the past is not as buried as we believe. The reason you and Sean worry about each other's previous significant others is that you realize the power they can still hold over your emotions. However, as long as you are sure that your desire to stay friends with your ex-beaus is really just that, there shouldn't be a problem. You both need the freedom to maintain other friendships outside of your relationship. It sounds like you know what you want, and it's Sean, so make that clear to him and let him know that you need the same reassurance. The most essential ingredient in a relationship is trust.

Do you have questions about love? Write to:
Jenny Burgess or Jake Korman
c/o Daniel Weiss Associates
33 West 17th Street
New York, NY 10011

Don't miss any of the books in 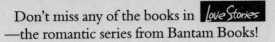 —the romantic series from Bantam Books!

DON'T MISS THE LATEST
Newbery Honor Book
by beloved author
PATRICIA REILLY GIFF

It is the summer of 1944 and World War II has changed almost everyone's life. Although Lily and her grandmother are at the family's cozy house on the Atlantic Ocean, Lily's summer does not appear promising. Her father has been sent overseas and her best friend has moved to a wartime factory town. But then Lily meets Albert, a refugee from Hungary with a secret sewn into his coat. When they join together to rescue and care for a kitten, they begin a very special friendship—but one that soon becomes threatened by lies.

0-385-32142-2

Now available from Delacorte Press

Real *life.*
Real *friends.*
Real *faith.*

Introducing Clearwater Crossing—

Where friendships are formed, hearts
come together, choices have consequences,
and lives are changed forever...

#2   0-553-57121-4

#1   0-553-57118-4

clearwater
crossing

Bantam Doubleday Dell
Books for Young Readers

BFYR 160